FLEECED

Also by Ellie Irving:

For the Record
Billie Templar's War
The Mute Button

FLEECED

ELLIE IRVING

CORGI BOOKS

FLEECED
A CORGI BOOK 978 0 552 56836 4

Published in Great Britain by Corgi Books,
an imprint of Random House Children's Publishers UK
A Penguin Random House Company

Penguin
Random House
UK

This edition published 2015

1 3 5 7 9 10 8 6 4 2

Copyright © Ellie Irving, 2015
Cover illustration copyright © Hannah Shaw, 2015

Penguin Random House is committed to a sustainable future
for our business, our readers and our planet. This book is made
from Forest Stewardship Council® certified paper.

MIX
Paper from
responsible sources
FSC® C018179

Set in Bembo 13/19½pt by Falcon Oast Graphic Art Ltd.

Corgi Books are published by Random House Children's Publishers UK,
61–63 Uxbridge Road, London W5 5SA

www.**randomhousechildrens**.co.uk
www.**totallyrandombooks**.co.uk
www.**randomhouse**.co.uk

Addresses for companies within The Random House Group Limited can be found at:
www.randomhouse.co.uk/offices.htm

THE RANDOM HOUSE GROUP Limited Reg. No. 954009

A CIP catalogue record for this book is available from the British Library.

Printed and bound in Great Britain by CPI Group (UK) Ltd, Croydon, CR0 4YY

For Lily Rose Irving

FLEECE

Noun

1. The woolly covering of a sheep or goat; the wool shorn from a sheep in a single piece at one time.

2. A soft warm fabric with a texture similar to sheep's wool, used as a lining material.

Verb

3. To obtain a great deal of money from someone, typically by overcharging or swindling them.

CHAPTER ONE

Charlie Rudge's whole life changed the day his dad won a sheep in a bet. He started off his morning with no sheep, and then his dad spent three hours in the Golden Fleece pub, and that evening there was a fully grown ewe tied to one end of the sofa in his living room, chewing her way through his mum's collection of Lisa Jewell novels.

No one could remember *exactly* what the bet was. It might have been an arm-wrestling contest. It could have been an adrenalin-fuelled game of tiddlywinks. Most likely it was a thumb war. Charlie's dad had larger-than-average thumbs. He could start World War Three with those bad boys.

Either way, Mr Hoskins from a nearby farm had decided to take on Mr Rudge, and Charlie had been woken that night by the sound of his dad crashing round the front room with Bertha the sheep under his arm.

Charlie's mum wasn't sure they could keep Bertha. (To be honest, she was miffed about the Lisa Jewell books.) But Charlie's dad said that if they were going to make a real go of this farming lark, if they were going to make the decision to leave their old lives in Southend and become farmers in Scotland, they had to have at least *one* animal on their farm.

So Bertha stayed.

The next morning, Mr Hoskins had come to the farm with his tail between his legs and tried to take the sheep back, but Charlie's dad said he'd won her fair and square, and showed Mr Hoskins the piece of paper they'd both scrawled their signature on the night before. So Bertha the sheep was now officially the property of the Rudge family, of Argonaut Farm, Ovwick Rumble, Scotland.

The Rudge family – Mum, Dad, Uncle Martin and Charlie, aged ten and three-quarters (plus Charlie's nineteen-year-old brother, Jimmy, but he wasn't ever going to move to Scotland, and so the less said about him, the better) – had only been farmers for a few weeks. Charlie's dad had received a letter from a solicitor saying that he and Martin were to inherit Argonaut Farm from their long-lost great-aunt. She was so long-lost, they didn't even know they *had* a great-aunt. But the solicitor's letter clearly read:

Dear Mr Michael Rudge,

It befalls Walters, Sloane, Walters, Walters, Sloane, Sloane and Walters (please bear with us – our business name is currently the subject of a legal dispute) to inform you that you and your brother, Martin Rudge, are the heirs to Argonaut Farm, previously the property of Cornelia Rudge, who has recently passed away. We are reliably informed that she was your great-aunt on your father's side. And yes, she knew you'd never kept in touch, but that's because she kept herself to herself and was ninety-seven and could only see out of one eye and couldn't stand Southend. But seeing as she had no other family and very much wanted the farm to continue to be run by a Rudge, as it has been for

*over two hundred years, Argonaut Farm was, upon
her death, passed to you.*

Yours sincerely,
Kevin Sloane-Walters and
Alicia Walters-Walters-Sloane

So Mum gave up her job behind the make-up counter in Debenhams and Dad gave up his job as a double-glazing salesman and Uncle Martin gave up his job as one of those people who stand on street corners with a sign saying GOLF SALE THIS WAY and Charlie gave up his paper round, and they moved up to Scotland to start a new, rural life.

Charlie had found it hard to leave Southend. Quite literally, for they'd been stuck in traffic on the A127 for three hours.

His parents had thrown a farewell party for all his friends, and they'd played one last game of footie in his back garden; Sam in goal, like he always was, Lucy, Rashid and Jesse on the wing, Rocky cutting up the oranges for half time, and Charlie out front, the best striker his team had ever had – almost as good as his all-time favourite football player, Alan Shearer.

The Rudges had packed up all their stuff and heaved all their worldly goods into the back of a removal van. Uncle Martin had been extra careful and insisted on holding his most prized possession, a limited-edition-mint-condition-never-to-be-opened Michael Bublé doll, in his lap the whole way there. Charlie's mum had been extra careful and insisted that all Jimmy's stuff, which had been confined to the loft these past two years, was carefully stowed in the removal van, but she'd had the sense not to let Charlie's dad know it.

Argonaut Farm was a small farm, as farms go. The farmhouse was a crumbling old stone building, with three bedrooms, a rustic and homely living room with peeling wallpaper, a kitchen with a dirty stove and a larder full of spiders, and an avocado-coloured bathroom. Two acres of land surrounded the farm, housing rusty garden chairs and a rusty table and, in the far corner, an unstable, three-legged chicken coop. Beyond the farmyard, there were two stables which would be most excellent for horses, should the Rudges choose to get some. There was also a disused potting shed at the very back of the farm, a barn, which would be most excellent for animals, and a tea room.

Charlie's mum spent the first week painting the living room and connecting the electricity. Uncle Martin spent the first week cleaning out the tea room, for he'd bagsied the role of running it. Charlie's dad spent the first week testing out the local takeaways.

Charlie had spent the first week in his new home trying to find someone to have a kick-about with, because his mum, dad and Uncle Martin were always busy. There weren't even any animals to ask. After a few days of moping round and kicking his football against the barn wall, Charlie's mum and dad had uttered the dreaded word 'school', and Charlie had pootled off to his first day at Ovwick Rumble Primary.

The school was located on the edge of the village and Charlie had to walk across three fields, climb over two stiles and hop across a narrow stream to get there. There was only one teacher, one classroom and six (now seven) children in the school, which was actually a Portakabin, because Ovwick Rumble was just about the smallest village in Scotland.

On his first day, after the teacher had introduced him as 'Charlie from Southend-on-Sea', Charlie had sat quietly at the back of the Portakabin, taking everything in, wondering what his old friends were doing. Playing footie, probably. Having a laugh, no doubt. At lunch time, he'd sat on his own on the bench in the playground, eating the cheese scone Uncle Martin had packed in his lunchbox, and he'd watched the other children tear around the yard playing a game of 'It'.

After a while, Charlie put down his scone. 'Can I play?' he called.

A scrawny, blond-haired boy took one look at him and said, 'Not if we can catch those,' and he pointed to Charlie's freckles.

Charlie sighed.

'Go on, Saul, let him,' said a short, dark-haired boy, but the blond boy ignored him.

Charlie huffed and reached inside his rucksack. He produced his football. 'What about a kick-about, then?' he said. 'I don't mind going in goal—' But the others had started chasing each other around the playground again.

Then the bell had rung and everyone had trudged back inside the Portakabin for afternoon lessons, and when it came to getting into pairs to do equivalent fractions for numeracy hour, nobody had wanted to work with the new boy with the freckly face. So Charlie had sat there working out the problems all on his own and realizing that his number one problem was how utterly rubbish his new life in Ovwick Rumble was.

His mum, dad and Uncle Martin, however, were having the time of their lives being farmers. Even though they had only ever seen farms on TV programmes like *Countryfile* and *One Man and His Dog*, they'd started to get the farm into some sort of order.

They'd cleaned out the cow shed and ordered two cows on the internet.

They'd bought three spades and a rake, and they'd circled a page in a catalogue to highlight the tractor they wanted to buy.

They'd adopted a dog – a scruffy black-and-white collie that they found wandering round the stables, with no collar or tag to show whether or not she belonged to anyone – and called her Bessie, planning to train her as a sheepdog.

They were becoming farmers.

And then, two weeks later, Dad had won Bertha in that bet, and Charlie had thought, 'At last! A five-a-side football team! If you count me, Mum, Dad and Uncle Martin, and I can get them all to stop for five minutes and play!' However, he quickly found out that Bertha was rubbish at footie, even in goal. She'd just stand there, chewing grass, while Charlie kicked the ball at her.

But *then* the Rudge family found out that Bertha was pregnant, and that's when everything – including this story – kicked off.

CHAPTER TWO

On the last day of April, in the midst of lambing season, Charlie noticed that Bertha was quiet. She didn't touch the food he gave her, and didn't scramble out of the way like she normally did when Bessie came bounding over, and they realized – at two o'clock in the morning, when Bertha started bleating and baaing so loudly they could hear her from the farmhouse – that she was about to have a lamb.

Because the Rudges were new to farming, Mr Hoskins decided to put aside his grudge over losing Bertha in the bet, and help Charlie's dad with his very first lambing. So did old Mrs Morrison, who owned the farm next door, and nine other farmers from in and around the village of Ovwick Rumble, in fact. They were eager to see what this new family from Southend who didn't have a clue about farming were up to.

With all the farmers and Charlie's mum, dad and Uncle Martin crowded into the barn, it seemed to Charlie like this was the most important birth anyone had ever witnessed. It was like the Nativity at Christmas. Except no one had bothered to bring the Rudges any gold, frankincense or myrrh.

Charlie watched, bleary-eyed but excited, as his dad pulled on a pair of long rubber gloves – the sort that make a pleasant kind of *SLLLLLLURRRRRPP* when you put them on. Slowly, slowly, slowly, he pulled a lamb – and gloop and blood and other nasty stuff that comes out of a sheep when they give birth – from Bertha.

Everybody went, 'Ooooooh!' and 'Aaaaaaaaah!' as the lamb shot out. And one person shouted, 'Oh, for the love of God!' but that was mainly because he was looking at the football scores on his phone at the same time.

The lamb lay on the floor next to its mother,

still covered in slime, and for a moment Charlie was sure it was dead. But then Bertha licked the lamb on its head, and it jumped into life, shakily standing on its hooves and wobbling around in a circle. Charlie let out a sigh of relief, realizing he'd been holding his breath all this time. The lamb was OK. Argonaut Farm's first animal success! They were proper farmers after all!

'It's a girl!' someone in the crowd shouted.

Charlie watched as the lamb shakily moved to the side of its mother, and started nudging at her stomach.

Charlie noticed Mr Hoskins deep in conversation with Mrs Morrison and a huddle of other farmers, all eyeing up the lamb suspiciously. He tugged on Mrs Morrison's jacket. 'Is everything all right?' he asked, worried.

Mrs Morrison broke out of the huddle and nodded, looking thoughtfully at the newborn lamb. 'A right beauty you've got there,' she said to Charlie. 'Just look at her fleece! I've never seen anything like it. Aye, that lamb's one in a million, you mark my words.'

And it was while Mrs Morrison and Mr Hoskins and all the other farmers who had come to see this birth were shaking hands and slapping Charlie's dad on his back and saying things like, 'Och, your first lambing season, well done, Mick, welcome to the club,' that Charlie noticed something strange about Bertha.

She wasn't breathing.

The lamb was trotting shakily on its legs again now, walking all around Bertha's body, nudging her, trying to get her to move.

Charlie caught Mrs Morrison's eye. He saw the frown on her face and watched as she strode over to Bertha and checked her vital signs. Charlie's dad quickly followed, kneeling beside her, biting his lip in worry.

After a moment, Mrs Morrison shook her head. 'She's dead,' she said softly. 'I'm sorry.'

The barn fell silent.

Mr Hoskins let out a sigh. 'Och, she was a fine sheep, was Bertha,' he said. He shook his head, eyed the newborn lamb one last time, and then left the barn.

Charlie wiped his face with his pyjama sleeve. The farmers and spectators all drifted away. Someone fleetingly placed a comforting hand on his shoulder, but then was gone.

When it was only Charlie and his dad left, Charlie's dad cradled Bertha in his arms. 'I'm sorry, Charlie,' he sighed. 'That's the circle of life for you.' He nodded to the lamb. 'But we'll call her yours, if you like? Your very own.' He shifted the dead sheep in his arms. 'We'll get more sheep, too, you'll see, so she won't be lonely. And you, Charlie Rudge, can be in charge of the sheep on this farm, how does that sound?' He shot Charlie a tight smile and strode out of the barn.

The lamb trembled in the space where Bertha had been. Charlie walked over to her and smoothed a hand over her still-slimy back.

'The circle of life,' Charlie repeated to himself. He knew all about that, and not just the song from *The Lion King*. He knew that lambs were born in the spring. He knew that pigs and cows and chickens were bred to be eaten. He knew that every animal and every person dies at one point or another. He couldn't learn to live on a farm without at least knowing *that*.

Bertha had been a Blackface ewe, one of the oldest breeds of sheep in Scotland, as Mr Hoskins had moaned the day he'd tried to get Bertha back. Her fleece had been white and her face had been black and that was pretty much that. This lamb, like her mother, was also a Blackface ewe, but, as Mrs Morrison had pointed out, she *was* different.

She had the same black face as Bertha, with tiny little horns curling around her ears. But her fleece was truly beautiful. A large black swirl swooshed over both sides of her body, breaking up the pure white wool. Her markings looked like the middle of a jam roly-poly pudding, curling round and round.

Charlie looked down at the lamb and vowed, there and then, to look after her. Bertha had been their first animal and Charlie would look after her daughter like the one-in-a-million sheep Mrs Morrison said she was. A boy with a face full of freckles and a sheep with a black-and-white fleece. They would be the best of friends.

'Alan Shearer,' he said out loud. It was the name

he'd been planning for the three hours it had been since they'd found out Bertha was pregnant. And the lamb's markings were the exact same colour as Newcastle's strip, where Alan Shearer used to play. It felt right.

Alan Shearer. Even though she was a she.

Maybe this Alan Shearer would be good at football, too.

And the lamb let out a little bleat; a 'BAAAAA', as if agreeing with him.

So Alan Shearer it was.

CHAPTER THREE

The next day, the most remarkable thing happened. Uncle Martin had run through the house at the crack of dawn, yelling 'MAYDAY! MAYDAY!' like he always did on the first day of May. Which hadn't gone down particularly well, seeing as everyone was so tired from being up half the night. But that wasn't what was remarkable. What was remarkable was the fact that there were customers in the tea room. Customers!

Admittedly, this is not remarkable for most tea rooms. Staff at The Ritz wouldn't have batted an eyelid.

But for Argonaut Farm, as run by the Rudges, it was the first chance they'd had to prove themselves.

At four o'clock that spring afternoon, just as

Charlie got back from school, a plump, blonde-haired woman dressed in wellies and a blue anorak dragged a scrawny, blond-haired boy into the tea room as if it were the most normal thing in the world.

Uncle Martin leaped to attention and thrust a menu at her. 'Welcome to Argonaut Farm Tea Room,' he said and made a little flourish with the corner of his pinny. 'Today's specials are apricot jam, apricot spread, apricot scones, apricot croissants, apricot iced fingers . . .' He smiled apologetically. 'We got a job lot of apricots.'

The woman crinkled her nose. 'My son would like to see the lamb,' she said.

Uncle Martin's eyebrows shot up. 'She's not on the menu,' he stuttered.

The woman smiled at him. 'Not to eat, dear thing,' she said, and looked at Uncle Martin like he was the daftest man she'd ever met. 'In the barn, is she?' the woman asked, looking about her.

'You want to see the sheep?' Uncle Martin said, not quite sure what was going on. 'You don't want any scones?'

The woman nodded, and clutched her son's hand.

'Right,' Uncle Martin sighed, his dream of working the till and hearing it pinging for real, actual customers rapidly slipping away. 'Follow me.'

Charlie was in the barn, tending to his new best friend. Normally sheep suckle at their mothers for milk, but seeing as the circle of life had claimed Bertha, that task now fell to Charlie. Charlie's dad had found a bottle in the kitchen, the sort of bottle used to feed babies, and Charlie now held it to Alan Shearer's mouth, stroking her as she gulped down the milk.

He looked up as the door opened. Uncle Martin stood in the doorway, his huge frame taking up the entire space. The blond-haired boy darted out from behind him and ran over to the sheep.

'Saul?' Charlie took a sharp intake of breath, startled. 'What are you doing here?'

Saul hadn't said anything at school that day about coming to Charlie's farm. But then, Saul hadn't said *anything* to Charlie since Charlie had started going to Ovwick Rumble Primary school.

Charlie didn't know what his problem was.

Saul dropped to his knees beside Alan Shearer. Alan Shearer backed away a little. Charlie didn't blame her, but he struggled not to let go of the bottle, or the scruff of her neck.

Saul looked Alan Shearer up and down, and reached out a hand to stroke her wool. 'It's proper rare,' he said, looking back to his mother for approval. 'Isn't it, Mum? Her fleece? Like "Best in Show" rare?'

Saul's mum pursed her lips. 'Come on, now,' she said. 'Time to be getting back. Your father will be wondering where we are.'

Saul got to his feet. He stared down at Charlie and Alan Shearer for a moment, frowning. 'You're not proper farmers,' he hissed at Charlie. 'You haven't got a clue. The sooner you go back to Southend, the better.'

Charlie opened his mouth to say something, but Saul ran back to his mum, and together they walked out of the barn.

'We'll be seeing you, Mr Rudge,' the woman said.

Uncle Martin ran after them, unable to let them go. 'Apricot éclair?' he shouted at them, following them down the dirt path from the barn and across the farmyard. 'Apricot macaroon?' he yelled as they lifted up the latch on the front gate and waltzed through it. 'Apricot tart?' But it was no good – his first ever customers, his first ever *sniff* of a tea-room sale, had gone.

Charlie sat in the barn for a moment more. Alan Shearer had finished her feed and was resting on the bed of hay beside him. Charlie stroked her fleece. It *was* beautiful, with those two swirling black swooshes. Saul hadn't made fun of Alan Shearer's markings, had he? But *rare*? Charlie didn't know about that. All sheep had a fleece, didn't they? The question was whether they had a fleece like Alan Shearer's.

Alan Shearer let out a little bleat just then. Charlie nodded. 'I know,' he confided to her. 'He's *not* very nice, is he? I guess he doesn't think we belong here. He doesn't say anything to me at school. Doesn't let me join in with anything. Doesn't want to play football. There's only seven of us. I've managed to avoid it so far, but I'm sure we'll definitely be paired up for something in the future. Imagine if I have to do assembly with him. Imagine if I have to do country dancing with him!'

Charlie winced at the thought.

Just then, Uncle Martin popped his head round the door, bleating something about apricot brownies, and Charlie kissed Alan Shearer on the top of her head and raced across the farmyard for his tea.

CHAPTER FOUR

A week had passed since Alan Shearer's birth. The Rudges held a little funeral service for Bertha, and buried her in the furthest field by the disused potting shed. Uncle Martin printed off a poem from the internet about stopping all the clocks, and wore one of Bessie's dog collars around his neck so he could pretend to be a vicar.

Charlie had visited Alan Shearer three times a day and every night to give her a milk bottle. Charlie's mum had tried once, because she said it reminded her of when her boys were babies, but then she got a bit teary and had to leave the barn. She said it was because the hay was making her sneeze, but Charlie knew better than that. Any time she thought about Jimmy, Mum got a bit teary.

Charlie's dad, however, had been spurred on by his success in delivering Alan Shearer, and had purchased nine new animals for the farm. Everyone had a say in what to call them. After much to-ing and fro-ing, the Rudges had named their new animals:

- David Beckham, Muhammad Ali, Jessica Ennis-Hill and Maria Sharapova, the sheep
- John Terry and Lance Armstrong, the chickens
- Babe Ruth and Laura Trott, the pigs

The two cows ordered over the internet had finally turned up, and were duly named Messi and Ronaldo, and Uncle Martin had got his way and named the new duck Michael Bublé, even though that wasn't in keeping with the general theme.

Argonaut Farm was beginning to flourish.

Before and after school that week, Charlie had tried to train Bessie into becoming a sheepdog, now that they had new animals – specifically sheep

– to round up. He'd bought a little tin whistle in the local post office and had studied videos on YouTube of all the noises and signals to command a sheepdog.

'Wheeet–wheeeo. Wheeet–wheeeo. Come by. Come by.'

That's the international command for a sheep-dog to turn in a clockwise direction when rounding up sheep.

At least, that's what a sheepdog's *meant* to do when they hear 'Wheeet–wheeeo. Wheeet–wheeeo. Come by. Come by.'

Bessie, it turned out, was quite possibly the worst sheepdog in the world. Turning in *any* direction when she heard 'Wheeet–wheeeo. Wheeet–wheeeo. Come by. Come by' would be a start. Even looking vaguely interested in *attempting* to round up the sheep would be *something*.

Instead, all Bessie would do was sit next to the sheep pen, looking up at Charlie in delight as he held his whistle to his lips and blew his commands, as pleased as punch to be there. How he was ever going to get her to lie in a field, then run towards the sheep and herd them in certain directions like a sheepdog was meant to do, he had no idea.

After trudging home from another rubbish day at Ovwick Rumble Primary, Charlie dumped his rucksack in the porch, plucked his tin whistle from where it was hanging by its rope on a hook on the wall, and headed across the farmyard for that day's 'Make Bessie a Sheepdog' attempt.

As he approached the barn, Charlie thought he could hear strange noises. A series of bangs and clatterings came from inside, followed by someone saying, 'Ooof, watch it, lad!' He approached cautiously, his whistle to his lips, ready to signal for help like an old-fashioned bobby on the beat.

And there, inside the barn, Mr Hoskins was straddling the gate of the sheep pen, one leg either side of it, trying to clamber down onto solid ground, with Alan Shearer tucked under his arm. And next to him, reaching up to help, was Saul.

'Hurry up, Dad,' Saul hissed. 'Someone will hear us.'

It took Charlie a moment to take everything in. He hadn't realized that this Mr Hoskins was

Saul's dad! And here they were trying to nick Alan Shearer!

'Someone *has* heard you,' Charlie said, glaring at them. 'What do you think you're doing?'

Saul's jaw dropped open when he realized they'd been caught in the act. Mr Hoskins looked at Charlie in panic. Alan Shearer started wriggling in his arms, like she knew she was being stolen.

Charlie craned his neck and yelled, 'Mum! Dad! Uncle Martin!'

'Now, now,' Mr Hoskins said hastily. 'Me and Saul here, we're just trying to claim what's rightfully ours.'

'What are you talking about?'

Mr Hoskins wiped his forehead with his free arm. All this stealing of sheep and straddling of sheep pens was clearly hot and bothering work. 'Bertha was my sheep. You know that,' he said slowly. 'Your dad won her in a bet, all right, fine. I meant what I said, she was a fine sheep. But this – her . . .' He nodded to Alan Shearer.

'She does have a name,' a deep voice suddenly piped up from behind Charlie. Uncle Martin moved into the barn, wearing his floral tea-room pinny and brushing flour from his already-greying hair.

Mr Hoskins glared at Charlie and Uncle Martin. 'You have no idea,' he hissed. 'No idea what you're dealing with here.'

Saul sneered at Charlie. 'Yeah,' he taunted. 'This sheep's worth a fortune. Like, megabucks.'

'Saul!' Mr Hoskins barked, and Saul clapped his hand over his mouth like he shouldn't have said that.

'I meant,' he stuttered, searching for words, 'she's worth a fortune 'cos she's gonna help me win the Young Farmer of the Year competition at the end of the month. Look at her fleece! She'll be crowned Best in Show, for sure. So deal with it.'

This was, quite frankly, the most that Saul had ever said to Charlie. 'That's why you wanted to see Alan Shearer the other day,' Charlie said, his mind whirring. 'So you could see if she was worth stealing or not.'

Saul looked to his dad and the still-struggling Alan Shearer. 'She belongs to me,' he said, 'and that's all there is to it.'

Uncle Martin stepped forward. 'I don't think so.'

Mr Hoskins and Saul both gulped. Uncle Martin may have been wearing a floral pinny, but he was also six foot four and looked like he played rugby for England.

'Mick won Bertha fair and circle,' Uncle Martin said. He often got his words mixed up, too, but everyone always knew what he meant. 'You signed a piece of paper, and everything.'

Mr Hoskins shifted his weight on top of the sheep-pen gate. 'Actually,' he started, 'I've had a word with my lawyers about that. Walters, Sloane, Sloane and – no, what was it? Sloane, Walters and Walters have said – no, it's Sloane, Walters—'

'Dad!' Saul cut in, exasperated. 'Their name isn't important right now.'

'No,' Mr Hoskins agreed. 'No, that's right. The point is, when things are won in a bet – a bet made after a pint of beer, at that—'

'Or six,' Saul sulked under his breath, but everyone heard him.

'Legally,' Mr Hoskins ploughed on, 'legally, who that thing belongs to is a grey area. And if that thing then has a lamb, well, legally, it's a minefield who really owns that. A minefield.'

Uncle Martin shook his head. 'I don't know about no legal things,' he said, 'but I do know that this sheep is ours, and that's all there is to it.' He thought for a moment. 'And we haven't got any minefields on Argonaut Farm.'

Charlie, Uncle Martin, Mr Hoskins and Saul all stood in silence for a few moments, glaring at one another, no one moving. They'd reached a stalemate. An impasse. Charlie didn't know what to do.

And then:

'Charlie? Is everything OK?'

Charlie thought he recognized that voice, but no – it couldn't be.

He'd not heard that voice in for ever.

Charlie turned round slowly and there, standing in the doorway of the barn like it was the most normal thing in the world, more normal than a tea room with customers, was Jimmy.

His brother.

The brother who hadn't lived with them for

two years since he'd stolen a car and run away with it. Well, *driven* away with it, if you want to get technical.

The brother who was well and truly the bad apple of the Rudge family, at any rate. And now here he was, as real as lamb chops, standing before him.

'Oh, blimey,' Charlie whispered.

'BAAAAA,' Alan Shearer bleated, even though she didn't know the half of it.

CHAPTER FIVE

*C*harlie ran forward and enveloped Jimmy in a hug. He didn't care what his mum and dad might say, all he knew was that he hadn't seen his brother in an awfully long time, and he'd missed him.

Mr Hoskins took the opportunity to clamber down from the sheep-pen gate, Alan Shearer still in his arms. He motioned to Saul to sneak round the side of the pen, but Uncle Martin was there like a shot, glaring menacingly at them, though Charlie knew Uncle Martin would never hurt a fly. Unless that fly had landed on a scone and Uncle Martin hadn't seen it, and he'd accidentally eaten it. Which had occurred on Day Two of Uncle Martin running the tea room, as it happens.

'Put. The. Sheep. Down,' Uncle Martin hissed and took a flour-dusted rolling pin from the pocket of his pinny. Mr Hoskins gulped again, but did what Uncle Martin said. He plonked Alan Shearer down on the ground and he and Saul backed away. 'You're an idiot,' Mr Hoskins whispered, 'who doesn't know what he's doing. Seventeen generations, my farm's been run by a Hoskins. We're Ovwick Rumble's most prominent farming family. What makes you think you can just waltz in here, taking a sheep that's rightfully mine?'

'That's as may be,' Uncle Martin replied. 'But *I'm* the one with the rolling pin.' And he whacked it against his palm for good measure.

Mr Hoskins and Saul gave one final huff, then slunk out of the back gate. 'And STAY OUT!' Uncle Martin yelled after them.

Then he turned to Jimmy and Charlie in the doorway. Jimmy looked anxiously at the rolling pin in Uncle Martin's hand. 'All right, Uncle Martin?' he gulped.

Uncle Martin put the rolling pin back in his pocket and opened his arms wide. 'Jimmy!' he cried. 'What a lovely surprise!' The two of them embraced while Charlie looked on. 'What brings you up here?'

Jimmy shrugged. 'I'd been doing a lot of thinking, while I was . . . away. Two years' worth of thinking. I missed you. That's all. I wanted to see you all again.'

Uncle Martin reached over and gave him another hug.

'Likely story,' a voice muttered behind them.

Everyone turned to see Charlie's mum and dad standing behind them. Charlie's mum placed her hand on his dad's arm. 'Come on now, Mick.' She turned to Jimmy and beamed at him. 'It's so good to see you again, love. Oh, look how you've grown!'

Charlie's dad snorted. 'He'll be after something, no doubt.'

Jimmy looked his dad square in the eye. 'I just wanted to see you all,' he repeated, calmly. 'Honestly. That's it. I figured, you all moved up here for a fresh start, so why can't I? I'm not after anything. Except, maybe, forgiveness.'

His mum ran over and hugged him. 'Oh, my love, of course. I got all your emails. Your dad read them, too. Didn't you, Mick? And Graham would fill us in on everything you'd been up to in between our visits. Are you hungry? Do you want a sandwich? I could make lasagne? Toast? What about a fry-up? Did you get the train up here?'

'Probably drove, knowing him,' Charlie's dad said under his breath, but Charlie heard him. 'And it wouldn't have been in his *own* car.'

Charlie's mum slung her arm round Jimmy's shoulders and walked him back towards the farmhouse, Uncle Martin following behind.

Charlie's dad looked at Alan Shearer, standing calmly outside the sheep pen. 'What's gone on here, then?' he asked Charlie.

'Mr Hoskins was trying to steal her,' Charlie replied. 'Along with his son Saul. He said that you might have won Bertha in a bet, but he'd been speaking to his solicitor, and apparently Bertha's lambs are a minefield, or something. He thought Alan Shearer belonged to him, at any rate. Saul said she's worth a fortune.'

Charlie's dad mulled this over, while Charlie opened the sheep-pen gate and shepherded Alan

Shearer back inside. Why Mr Hoskins had been straddling the sheep pen to steal her instead of just using the gate, Charlie did not know.

'Interesting,' Charlie's dad whispered to himself. 'Very interesting.'

'I'm glad Jimmy's back,' Charlie said to his dad. 'I haven't seen him in ages.'

His dad raised one eyebrow. 'Hmph,' he grunted by way of reply. 'Hmph.' Which was both helpful *and* conversational.

As his dad left the barn and followed the others back to the farmhouse, Charlie smoothed Alan Shearer's fleece and fluffed up her bed of hay and topped up her water bowl. She must have been rattled, with all this commotion going on.

'It's been two years, Alan,' Charlie whispered to her, conspiratorially. 'Jimmy stole someone's car and drove off along the seafront. Joyriding, the police called it. They let him off 'cos it was his first offence, but Mum and Dad had had it up to here with him, because he wasn't going to college like he was meant to and he was hanging out with some bad older boys like he *wasn't* meant to, so they sent him to live with Cousin Graham so he could learn a trade and stay out of trouble. I've only seen him a handful of times since.'

Alan Shearer bleated like she understood, but she didn't know how awkward that handful of meetings had been. The last time they'd seen Jimmy had been at Christmas. Charlie's dad had got lost on the way to Cleethorpes, Cousin Graham had forgotten they were even coming and hadn't ordered in any food, and Charlie's mum had got the fright of her life when she opened the wrong door in Cousin Graham's house and found herself in the embalming room, face-to-face with a corpse. Cousin Graham was an undertaker, you see. Even at Christmas.

'But we'll be a proper family again. The five of us.' Another thought popped into Charlie's head. The five-a-side football team! At last! No sheep need apply!

'You'll love Jimmy, Alan Shearer,' Charlie said, scraping mud and stray bits of hay off his trainers on the sheep-pen gate. 'He's brilliant. He's properly funny and daft, like Uncle Martin. But he's good at football, really good. Not as good as Alan Shearer, or anything. The other one. But good. You'll see.'

Charlie clicked the sheep-pen gate shut. 'We'll all be a proper family again, just like old times,' he said, grinning, and headed back towards the farmhouse, thinking how this had turned into one of the best days of his life. His brother had come back. He'd stopped a crook of a farmer and his horrible son from stealing his best sheep and friend. They were having a cooked breakfast for dinner and there were more apricot scones for dessert. It was definitely in his top five.

In the kitchen, Charlie's mum was preparing a feast fit for a king. Baked beans were being stirred in the saucepan; eggs were being fried in the frying pan; mushrooms, tomatoes and sausages were being grilled under the grill, and slices of brown bread, white bread, bloomer bread, granary bread, multi-seeded bread and Hovis 50/50 were all being buttered on the side. 'I'm not even that hungry,' Jimmy whispered to Charlie as he sat down at the kitchen table. Charlie grinned back at him.

Charlie's dad hovered behind them, pacing up and down the kitchen floor. 'Now, Jimmy,' he said, 'I expect you'll be wanting to move on shortly. If I know you, you'll want to make your own way in the world.'

Jimmy shrugged. 'I thought I could stay for a while. Help out. I'd pull my weight on the farm, you know that.'

'Go on, love,' Charlie's mum said to Charlie's dad. 'He'd be good on a farm.'

'What does that mean?' Charlie's dad asked, exasperated.

'Look how he's grown!' Charlie's mum replied. 'He's a strapping man now.' She turned from the stove to get a good look at Jimmy. He was taller, his hair darker, his skin more tanned, his arms stronger and more muscly, his grin wonkier since the last time they'd seen him. 'All handsome and everything,' she continued. 'He could muck out the horses, drive the tractor, that sort of thing.'

'We haven't got a tractor,' Charlie's dad snorted. 'Or any horses.' He was slightly miffed that Charlie's mum had never called *him* 'strapping' in his life. 'Stocky' and 'well built' were the sort of words she used to describe him. Also 'receding hairline'.

'Oh, you know what I mean. Who wants fried bread?'

Uncle Martin dished out the plates and cutlery as Charlie's mum went round the table dishing out the food, humming a little tune.

Charlie hadn't seen her this chirpy since, well, he couldn't quite remember when.

Charlie's dad folded his arms. 'We should at least discuss this as a family.'

'That's what we're doing now,' Uncle Martin said matter-of-factly as he reached for the tomato ketchup. 'My vote is: Jimmy can stay.'

'Me too,' Charlie piped up through a mouthful of sausage. Jimmy gave him a grateful smile.

'Me three,' Charlie's mum laughed, doling out an extra heap of baked beans on Jimmy's already-heaving plate. 'You know Cousin Graham told us how well Jimmy did staying with him. How helpful he was round the house. How good he was with the law.'

Charlie's dad arched an eyebrow. 'Just because someone has managed to avoid getting into trouble with the police for two years after stealing a car and joyriding down Southend seafront does not make them "good with the law".'

Uncle Martin, Charlie, Charlie's mum and Jimmy

all looked at Charlie's dad, who was standing, arms folded, to one side of the kitchen.

'Please?' Charlie whispered. 'I want to have my brother back.'

Charlie's dad opened his mouth to say something, but then thought better of it. He looked around at each of them, before finally nodding his head. 'Fine,' he sighed. 'Fine. Jimmy can stay. But he's got to help out round the farm. He's got to pull his weight, just like everyone does at Argonaut. And if there's even the slightest hint of trouble, young man, if I get one whiff of law-breaking or—'

'You won't, Dad,' Jimmy interrupted. 'I promise.'

Charlie's dad unfolded his arms and scraped back a chair. 'Right, well, then. That's settled.'

Charlie's mum leaned over and kissed her husband on the cheek. 'Thanks, love. Eggy bread?'

'Ah, go on, then. Eggy bread.'

And just like that, Charlie had his whole family back.

But the good times weren't to last for long, else this wouldn't be much of a story.

CHAPTER SIX

Charlie's mum put up a rickety old camp bed she found in the attic and Jimmy spent the night in Charlie's room. It felt just like old times. In Southend they'd shared a room, though Charlie had had it to himself for the past two years.

Charlie had wanted to talk to Jimmy about everything – Cleethorpes, Southend, his mates, who he'd kept in touch with, what he thought of the farm, how many apricot scones he'd eaten – but Jimmy had said the journey from Cleethorpes to Scotland had taken it out of him, and he'd gone to sleep as soon as his head hit the pillow.

The next morning, after a breakfast of now slightly stale apricot scones, Charlie reached for Uncle Martin's laptop.

He'd been thinking and thinking, ever since the Great Sheep Rustling Incident the day before. Saul had said that he wanted to steal Alan Shearer because she was going to win a competition for him, but Charlie hadn't had a clue what he'd meant.

Charlie opened the laptop and typed 'Best in Show' into the search engine. He scrolled down, through pages about a *Best in Show* film and a *Best in Show* dog contest, and then a page popped up with the heading SCOTTISH YOUNG FARMER OF THE YEAR COMPETITION. Charlie clicked the link and eagerly read through the information.

Each year, on the last Sunday in May, farmers under the age of fourteen from all over Scotland got together and competed in a series of farming tasks, winning points for each round. These tasks consisted of:

Fastest time to roll a bundle of hay
Driving a tractor round an obstacle course which
    includes a hoop of fire
Most milk milked from a cow
Best sheepdog at rounding up sheep

Loudest oink from a pig

Fastest person to find a needle in a haystack

Sheep-shearing

And, just as Saul had said, every year there was a Best in Show section for the final round, where the contestants had to bring the best sheep from their farms to show off and help them win the crown.

Charlie closed the laptop. He'd made a decision. He would enter the competition. Because with a fleece like hers, Alan Shearer would stamp all over the other contestants. And that would show everyone. That would show Saul Hoskins.

He sensed someone hovering behind him, and looked round to see Jimmy grinning. He held out his hand and hoisted Charlie from his chair. 'Like old times?' he said.

Charlie knew immediately what he meant. He shoved on his wellies, and raced after Jimmy. Together they ran out of the farmhouse, across the farmyard, sending the chickens scattering, through the back field of Argonaut Farm, past the empty stables and down the narrow dirt track.

Just like old times, Charlie thought to himself. Even though Charlie's memories of Jimmy over the years were hazy, the one thing he could always remember about him was running. Always running. Running on the football pitch at the local rec, running for the bus at the end of their road. Running away from the people Jimmy owed money to. That was another reason he was sent to live with Cousin Graham.

Jimmy's speciality was to take Charlie out for a milkshake, or a burger and fries, and never pay. He always chose a diner or café, never a McDonald's or anywhere where you had to pay *before* you got your food. And then, once they'd had their diet Cokes, or banana smoothies, or hot dogs, or ice creams, Jimmy would tell Charlie to wait outside while he paid up. Then he'd wait until the waitress went off to get their bill, and leg it outside. He'd grab Charlie's hand and the pair of them would run down the street, more often than not being chased by an angry waiter, or manager, or fellow customer.

Charlie never asked Jimmy why he didn't just pay like normal people did, but he suspected it was something to do with the thrill of it all. That was why Jimmy had stolen the car and driven recklessly down Southend seafront, after all. Charlie never liked doing a runner, though. He always felt bad for the poor waitress who had to explain to her manager why their takings were short that afternoon. Still, it meant spending time with Jimmy, and that's all Charlie ever really wanted.

Charlie and Jimmy caught their breath somewhere by the barn. Jimmy placed his hands on his knees and inhaled long, sharp breaths. 'Woo!' he puffed. 'Been a while since I did that!'

'Did you never take Cousin Graham out for milkshakes, then?' Charlie asked, innocently enough.

Jimmy smiled, though there was something sad about the way he did it. 'Can't see Cousin Graham legging it down the road from a diner, can you?' he replied. His gaze wandered back to the farmhouse. 'Besides, I don't do that sort of thing any more.'

Charlie heaved the door to the barn open, and the smell hit them immediately. 'Cor!' Jimmy exclaimed, holding his nose. 'That's worse than Dad after he's had a curry!'

Charlie giggled and led Jimmy inside the barn. 'We've got two pigs now,' he said, pointing to them both. 'Babe Ruth and Laura Trott. Dad named them.'

Jimmy rolled his eyes. 'Of course he did.'

Charlie giggled again. 'You should hear what he's called the sheep.'

A loud buzzing sound rang out from Jimmy's pocket. He reached inside and pulled out his mobile phone. Charlie caught the look of annoyance on his face as he saw who was ringing him. Jimmy pressed 'ignore' and shoved the phone back in his pocket.

They stood looking at Babe Ruth and Laura Trott eating from their food trough for a little while in comfortable silence. Laura Trott was a Large Black, with droopy ears that nearly covered her entire face. Babe Ruth was a Yorkshire pig. Pink all over and exceptionally, exceptionally fat.

The loud buzzing sound rang out from Jimmy's pocket again. He took out his mobile and pressed 'ignore' once more.

'Don't you want to answer it?' Charlie asked.

Jimmy frowned. 'Don't worry about it.'

Charlie took a deep breath, and then asked the question he'd wanted to ask ever since he first saw Jimmy again. 'Do you think you're going to stick around?' he said. 'To stay for good?'

Jimmy looked Charlie over. 'Do you think?' Charlie repeated in a small voice. He crossed his fingers behind his back, hoping the answer would be a big, fat YES.

The loud buzzing sound rang out once more and Jimmy let out a small cry of anguish. 'For God's sake!' He pressed 'ignore' a third time.

'Is there a problem?' Charlie asked.

Jimmy tossed his mobile into the pigsty, where it landed under Babe Ruth's right trotter. The pig walked forward to snuffle at the trough once more, and the *CRUUUUUUUNCCCH* of the mobile phone being trampled echoed around the sty. Charlie and Jimmy looked at the phone as it lay in pieces.

'Not any more,' Jimmy said. He put his arm round Charlie's shoulders and the pair of them walked out of the barn. 'And in answer to your original question, yes, I plan to stick around for good.' He grinned at Charlie, who beamed right back at him.

That's when they heard the scream from the farmhouse.

'AAAAAAAAAAAAAAAARRRRGGGHHHH!'

It was a high-pitched scream, short and urgent. It sounded like a woman being strangled. Jimmy and Charlie looked at each other for a moment. 'Mum!' Jimmy cried. Then he tugged at Charlie's sleeve, and the pair of them ran, ran, ran for their lives across the farmyard.

CHAPTER SEVEN

Jimmy and Charlie burst through the kitchen door to find their parents in a state.

'What's going on?' Jimmy cried as their mum fanned their dad in the face with a tea towel. He was lying flat on the kitchen floor, dazed.

'Your dad's had a bit of a shock,' their mum replied. 'Nothing to worry about. He's—'

Mr Rudge sat bolt upright. 'We're rich!' he cried, batting the tea towel away from his head. 'We're only bleeding, stinking rich!'

Jimmy and Charlie exchanged a look of confusion. Just then, Uncle Martin burst through the kitchen door. 'Is everything OK?' he yelled. 'I heard a woman scream.'

'That was Dad!' Charlie giggled, while his dad looked on sheepishly.

Charlie's mum helped her husband stagger to his feet, and sat him down in a chair as everyone waited for an explanation. 'I started thinking, see,' Charlie's dad said, blinking around at everyone. 'Why would Mr Hoskins be so fussed about getting Alan Shearer back if she wasn't worth a few bob? Why did his wife and son come to the tea room that day? It wasn't for the scones.'

Uncle Martin frowned at this, but he didn't say anything.

'It was to check her fleece,' Charlie's dad continued. 'You were right, Charlie. Alan Shearer's worth a fortune!'

Charlie's mum handed her husband a glass of water, and he drank from it with shaky hands. 'Take it easy, Mick,' she warned. 'Your dad's been on the phone to Mr Partridge,' she said, turning to face Charlie and Jimmy. 'He runs a farm in Bovwick Ramble, the next town over. He's head of the Rural Association in Scotland, and he judges something

51

called the Young Farmer of the Year competition every year. He's official, like.'

Charlie's ears pricked up at that.

'And?' Uncle Martin asked, leaning forward in anticipation.

'And,' Charlie's mum explained, 'Mr Partridge said, from what he's heard, with her stock as a Blackface ewe and a fleece like no other sheep he knows of, Alan Shearer could be unique. One of a kind!'

Well, Charlie could have told anyone that.

Charlie's mum wasn't done. 'She's worth a fortune! Something to do with the breeding properties and quality of wool, or something, I didn't quite understand. I think they sell the wool to Harris Tweed. You know, those tweed suits people wear. You can get them in all sorts of colours. Green and yellow checks, if you like. Or maybe it was something to do with—'

'He's coming here,' Charlie's dad interrupted before his mum could bang on any more. 'Mr Partridge. Tomorrow. He's going to check Alan Shearer out and let us know once and for all.

He said he didn't want to get our hopes up, but we could be looking at something like sixty thousand pounds. Sixty thousand pounds! Imagine that!'

'Sixty thousand pounds?' Uncle Martin repeated.

'Sixty. Thousand. Pounds!' Charlie's dad looked like his five numbers and the bonus ball had just come up. Which wasn't far off. 'Think what we could do with this place with sixty thousand pounds! We could have horses, Martin. Lots of horses. And a tractor. Two tractors! We could turn this place into a petting zoo. We could get a llama!'

'A llama? In Scotland?' Charlie's mum asked, bemused. She looked around the rustic kitchen, with its worn carpet and heavy red curtains. 'We could spruce this place up. Venetian blinds, for starters.' She looked down at the pink wellies she'd been wearing ever since they'd moved up to Scotland. Her job in high heels behind the make-up counter in Debenhams seemed a lifetime ago. 'I could get new shoes.'

'I could get a Ferrari,' Jimmy said, grinning,

but no one seemed to find that funny.

'We'll have TWO tea rooms, Martin,' Charlie's dad continued, completely oblivious to anyone else's suggestions. 'That'll show everyone.' He and Uncle Martin reached across the table and shook hands in delight.

Charlie cleared his throat. 'Yeah, but you wouldn't sell her, would you?' he said.

His dad blinked at him in surprise. 'What?'

'Alan Shearer? It's not like you'd sell her. 'Cos she's mine. You said so. The night she was born. You said I could keep her, and be in charge of all the sheep. You said it.'

Charlie's dad looked sheepish again. 'Yes, well,' he blustered, 'that was before we knew how much she was worth.'

'But she's my friend,' Charlie said simply.

Charlie's dad frowned. 'There are no friends in business,' he said. 'That's the first thing you learn about in double glazing.' He thought for a moment. 'Actually, the first thing you learn about in double glazing is the BFRC rating system for energy efficient windows.' He thought for another moment. 'And *then* you learn about un-plasticized polyvinyl chloride.' He thought for a moment more. 'And *then* you learn how to bump up the prices. But yes, the fourth thing you learn about in double glazing, Charlie, is that there are no friends in business.'

Charlie looked at his family earnestly. 'I want to keep her,' he pleaded. 'I'd miss her so much if we sold her. Plus, Saul said that Alan Shearer would be sure to be crowned Best in Show at the Young Farmer of the Year competition, and I want to win it. I've decided to enter it, 'cos I want to be a proper farmer. I'd be a proper farmer if I won that, wouldn't I?'

'Yes, but—' his dad blustered again, once more lost for words. 'Yes, but—'

'But nothing,' Charlie's mum butted in. She moved to stand by Charlie and placed a hand on his shoulder. 'Charlie's right, Mick. Alan Shearer is his and that's all there is to it.'

The colour drained from Charlie's dad's face. 'Sixty. Thousand. Pounds,' he whispered.

'There'll be other sheep, Dad,' Jimmy said.

'Not like this!' he spluttered.

Uncle Martin shook his head and said firmly, 'Mick, Rachel's right. Charlie's right. Jimmy's right. Alan Shearer is not to be sold.'

And so that was that.

That night before bed, Charlie went down to the barn to give Alan Shearer her evening feed. It wouldn't be much longer until they could wean her off the bottle and onto solid grass. She was still a small slip of a thing, but her fleece had grown in the few weeks since her birth, and was by now a couple of centimetres thick. It seemed whiter, somehow, and the black swirl of her markings more pronounced. But maybe it just seemed like that because now Charlie knew how special she was.

Charlie tucked his jeans into his wellies, pulled the zip of his fleece all the way up to his chin and sat down on the bale of hay next to Alan Shearer. She glugged at the milk bottle greedily, and Charlie soothed her head as she drank. 'Don't you worry, Alan Shearer,' he whispered to her. 'I'll make sure Dad never sells you.'

After he'd finished feeding her, Charlie went round and patted David Beckham, Muhammad Ali, Jessica Ennis-Hill and Maria Sharapova on their heads in turn, and plumped up their hay bales for the night. Maybe it was because Alan Shearer was the first and only animal to have been born on the farm that Charlie couldn't help but like her more than the others. Maybe it was because she *was* more special and rare than any other sheep. Charlie knew he probably shouldn't have favourites, but he just couldn't help it. He closed the sheep-pen gate, said good night to the rest of the animals housed in the barn, and sloped back across the farmyard, hoping all the while that this wasn't how his mum and dad felt about him and Jimmy, and if so, who was *their* favourite?

The next morning, Mr Partridge, the official farmer from the next town of Bovwick Ramble, came to Argonaut Farm to value Alan Shearer. Even though the Rudges knew she wasn't to be sold, Charlie's dad didn't think it would do business any harm if everyone knew how rare and valuable Argonaut

Farm's livestock was. They could make a feature out of it, Charlie's mum said, and advertise their famous animal, and she started typing 'HOW MUCH DOES IT COST TO PRINT A THOUSAND LEAFLETS?' into Google.

Mr Partridge spent a good half an hour looking at Alan Shearer. He didn't say anything as he walked round her, but grunted every now and then. He and Charlie's dad got on like a house on fire. Then he measured Alan Shearer's height and weight and length, and looked in her eyes, at her hooves, at her front legs and hind legs, under her belly and at her fleece.

The other sheep in the sheep pen didn't get a look-in.

After thirty agonizing minutes, Mr Partridge turned to the Rudge family and said, 'Excellent size, excellent head shape, excellent coat, excellent character,' which Charlie thought was a bit odd, seeing as he didn't even know Alan Shearer that well. 'She's a Blackface, all right. But what makes her worth a pretty penny is those markings of hers, make no mistake.'

Jimmy high-fived Charlie. Charlie's mum gave Charlie's dad a kiss on the cheek, but he just frowned. Uncle Martin bear-hugged Mr Partridge like there was no tomorrow, and it was only by Mr Partridge tapping him on the back seventeen times that Uncle Martin finally let go.

'So that's that, then! I'm bound to win now,' Charlie said.

'Win what?' Mr Partridge asked, packing away his tape measure and scales.

'Young Farmer of the Year,' Charlie answered. 'There's a Best in Show category, right?'

Mr Partridge smiled, knowingly. 'That would be telling,' he grinned. 'As Head Judge of the competition, I couldn't possibly be seen to be giving away insider information to you or any other young farmer, laddie.'

'Yeah, but Saul Hoskins said,' Charlie replied.

Mr Partridge nodded his head. 'I suppose it wouldn't be too indiscreet to tell you that, for the last fourteen years of the competition, in all the time I've been Head Judge, the final round has always been "Best in Show".' He tapped his nose conspiratorially. 'You mark my words, laddie. With that sheep on your side, you'll not go wrong.'

Charlie beamed at him, while Jimmy slapped him on the back in delight. His dad looked on, still with a frown, until Charlie's mum nudged him in the ribs and hissed, 'See? We're not selling him.'

Mr Partridge strode out of the sheep pen and Charlie trotted alongside him. 'Do you reckon Alan Shearer knows she's famous?' he said.

Mr Partridge stopped in his tracks and stared across the farm to the commotion that was occurring outside the tea room. 'I don't know about that,' he laughed. 'But I do know that news of your famous sheep has spread already.'

A line of people, at least ten in number, stood outside the tea room, waiting for service.

'Blimey!' Uncle Martin cried. You could practically see the ping of the till calling to him. 'MAYDAY! MAYDAY!' he yelled, and he raced past Mr Partridge to the tea room, holding his pinny aloft in excitement.

Mr Partridge shook Charlie's hand, and then went on his way.

He had been right. News of Alan Shearer *officially* being a rare sheep spread around the village of Ovwick Rumble in next to no time. By mid-afternoon, nineteen people had visited the tea room and enquired after the sheep. Uncle Martin had never been so busy making scones and serving tea.

And even though Charlie's dad knew once and for all that they would not be selling Alan Shearer, he was still happy that so many people had turned up to the farm. He calculated that, if this kept happening on a daily basis, and he started charging a £1 entry fee for people to have a look at Alan Shearer before they sampled the delights of the tea room, they'd have made the sixty thousand pounds in . . . however long it took for sixty thousand people to visit Argonaut Farm. By the end of the month, maybe?

Because it was so busy, and everyone had to pull their weight, Jimmy and Charlie volunteered to help out in the tea room and they quickly fell into their roles. Jimmy waited tables and took orders and served behind the till – though he had to let

Uncle Martin press the button that made the 'ping' noise; Charlie did the washing up in the kitchen, and Uncle Martin was to oversee everything, while replenishing the scones and cakes on display and re-filling the jam pots and butter bowls.

And it was while Charlie, Jimmy and Uncle Martin were running the tea room like a well-oiled operation that two strange things happened to Jimmy.

He was blackmailed by an ex-WWE wrestler whose hands were as big as meat cleavers.

He fell in love. Utterly, instantly, insanely, head-over-heels in lurve.

These two things were not related. Jimmy did not fall utterly, instantly, insanely, head-over-heels in lurve with an ex-WWE wrestler with meat cleavers for hands.

Still, it was *quite* the afternoon for him.

CHAPTER EIGHT

Eloise Grantham was a shy, eighteen-year-old girl who worked in Debbie & Dale's Dairy & Baked Goods Emporium in the village of Ovwick Rumble. Slim, petite and unassuming, she was the sort of girl you never really noticed was there. Dale, of Debbie & Dale's Dairy & Baked Goods Emporium had died three years previously in a tragic industrial accident involving a giant vat of butter and a churning machine, but Debbie, her daughter Eloise and Eloise's grandma, Madge, had kept the name Debbie & Dale's Dairy & Baked Goods Emporium because it gave a nice sense of continuity to the business. Also it saved having to print a new sign for the front door.

Ever the businesswoman, Debbie had decided

to foster relations between the Baked Goods Emporium and Argonaut Farm, and had sent Eloise along with a business card and a price list of goods offered.

When Eloise walked through the tea-room door that afternoon, her mousy brown hair blowing in the wind, carrying a welcome basket of tiger bread and salted pretzels, Jimmy locked eyes with her and his heart swelled. It was instantaneous. Love at first sight. He could hear light, angelic chimes ringing out all round him, as if angels were accompanying this vision of beauty straight to his door.

'Those wind chimes don't half get on your nerves,' Uncle Martin declared, nodding to the door, where wind chimes hung down and brushed against anyone entering the premises.

Eloise blushed as she passed Jimmy the basket of baked goods, the Debbie & Dale's Dairy & Baked Goods Emporium business card stuck prominently amongst the apple strudels.

'Th-thanks,' Jimmy stuttered, plonking the basket down on the counter by the till. 'I – I work here.'

The tea room was, like everything on Argonaut Farm, 'rustic', meaning that the walls were distressed, the tablecloths not from this century, and the crockery slightly chipped. There was enough room for nine tables, with chairs dotted around them, and a counter, which displayed Uncle Martin's apricot scones and housed a till on top.

At the back of the tea room was the kitchen, where Charlie was merrily washing up. Through the hatch in the wall he could see everything, and he laughed as Jimmy just stared and stared at the poor girl. Eloise blushed again and turned redder than Charlie's hair.

'Can you serve table three, please, Jimmy?' Uncle Martin hissed as he swiped the basket from the counter and headed back into the kitchen. 'Today?'

Eloise nodded goodbye and headed out of the tea room, back across the farmyard. Jimmy stood gazing out of the window at her until she was but a speck on the horizon.

'TODAY!' Uncle Martin bellowed through the hatch.

Jimmy gave a start and scrambled out from

behind the counter. He reached into his pocket and took out a little notepad and pencil, then headed over to table three.

'Welcome to Argonaut Farm. What can I get you, gentlem—' Jimmy gave a small cry when he saw the two men sitting there.

One was thin and wiry, with sharp, beady eyes and a thin black moustache. The other was a big brute of a man, with hair on his knuckles and a completely bald head, sitting squashed up with his knees under his chin on the too-small tea-room chair.

'What are you doing here?' Jimmy hissed, looking about him to check that neither Charlie nor Uncle Martin were in earshot.

The thin wiry man smiled, and placed the broadsheet newspaper he was reading on the table. 'You're an elusive man, Mr Rudge,' he sneered. 'Something wrong with your phone?'

Jimmy leaned down to him. 'What are you doing here?' he said again in a low voice.

The thin wiry man huffed. 'What do you expect when you don't answer our phone calls?'

Jimmy pocketed his notepad and pencil. 'Look, just leave me alone, all right? I mean it.'

The big brutish man cracked his knuckles. '*We* mean it too,' he said. Jimmy gulped.

'Brauns here can get very handy with his hands if we don't get what's owed to us,' the wiry man said. 'Just ask Mr Theodopolis. Oh, no, wait, you can't. He's currently *in hospital*.'

Jimmy raised an eyebrow. 'That's 'cos he got malaria on holiday. I heard about that. And *Brauns*? Seriously? You actually call him *Brauns*?'

The big brutish man – Brauns – nodded. 'He's Brains,' he said, motioning to the thin wiry man and his newspaper. ''Cos he's smart and clever and does crossword puzzles and things. And I'm Brauns, 'cos I like hitting people.' He picked up the pen Brains had been using for his crossword, and snapped it clean in two. 'And breaking things.'

Brains frowned. 'Yes, thank you, Brauns,' he said. 'I was two clues away from completing that.'

Jimmy gulped again. 'Right. Well. I haven't got any money.'

Brauns scraped back his chair.

'No! Wait! Wait!' Jimmy said quickly. He looked round again to check no one was paying any attention, but everyone was just busy eating their scones, or spreading butter on their bread, or gossiping about Alan Shearer. Jimmy sighed, and walked quickly over to the till.

He checked for a third time that neither Charlie nor Uncle Martin were looking, then opened the till and pulled out a couple of notes. 'That's all I've got,' he said in a low voice, thrusting the money at Brains.

Brains looked from Jimmy to the open till. 'It's not *all* you've got,' he replied, raising an eyebrow.

Jimmy shook his head firmly. 'No. I'm not stealing from my family. I'll have to pay this back from today's wages as it is. I'll get more, but you've got to give me time. I've got to earn the money, fair and square.'

Brains riffled through the notes, then folded them neatly and placed them in his pocket. 'Very well,' he said. 'We're staying in rooms above the pub in town. The Golden Fleece. And we're not going anywhere until we've got all of what you owe us.'

They waltzed out of the tea room. Jimmy closed the till, a sinking, sickly feeling in his stomach. And it wasn't just from Uncle Martin's now ridiculously stale apricot scones.

There was a buzz of excitement in the farmhouse that evening.

Charlie's dad was pleased that the farm was starting to get somewhere and was already thinking about plans for expansion. Uncle Martin was having a delightful time chatting online to a Michael Bublé fan with the username ILOVEMBUBL3 who was almost as obsessed as he was. And Charlie's mum was having a good day on her 5:2 diet.

Jimmy had given Charlie a book he'd found in the attic while sorting through the boxes of his possessions that their mum had brought up from Southend. It must have belonged to Cornelia Rudge, for it was a musty, dusty old hardback, with a picture of a pig on the front, and the title *Farming Today*. Charlie leafed through it, desperate for any information on how to be a farmer, and trying not to splodge any of his shepherd's pie onto the pages.

Only Jimmy was less than enthusiastic all evening. He didn't say anything when his dad asked him how well the tea room had done that day. He just shrugged when Charlie pointed out a page of sheepdog commands from the book. He only shook his head when their mum asked if he wanted more shepherd's pie. And when Uncle Martin gave Jimmy his wages from that afternoon, Jimmy didn't say a word. He put the money in his pocket and carried on pushing peas around his plate.

He didn't even say anything when his dad whispered, 'I've got my eye on you, son. Remember, at the first whiff of trouble . . .' across the table.

Instead, Jimmy smiled at his mum to thank her for dinner and said softly, 'I'm going to have an early night. It's been a long day,' and went upstairs to bed.

His mum shot his dad a look. 'What have you been saying to him? Have you been upsetting him, Mick?'

'Don't ask me,' Charlie's dad huffed, tucking into another helping of shepherd's pie.

★

That night, as Charlie lay in bed, he spent a few minutes listening to the sound of Jimmy sleeping on the camp bed on the other side of the room, the gentle rise and fall of his chest as he breathed.

'Thank you for my book, Jimmy,' Charlie whispered to him. 'It'll come in so handy for the competition. I'm really glad you came back. I'm really glad we're a proper family again. And I don't ever want you to go away again, all right? Ever.' He shut his eyes tight, rolled over, and went to sleep.

After a moment, Jimmy opened his eyes. He hadn't been able to sleep at all, but instead lay there, staring at the ceiling, thoughts whirring round and round his mind.

The men he owed money to had tracked him down to the family farm. Who knew how long they would keep quiet? Who knew how long they would give him before they started demanding more money? Or blood? Or both?

Where was he going to get that sort of cash from? He couldn't keep stealing from the tea-room till. It wasn't fair on his family.

He wiped a tear from his cheek, and stared into

the darkness, no idea how the heck he was going to get himself out of his latest predicament.

The next morning, Charlie was trying to enjoy a prolonged snooze before he had to get out of bed and trudge to school for another day of being ignored. He was just in the middle of a delightful dream about scoring the winning goal for Newcastle in the FA Cup when he was jolted awake by a loud banging on the front door. *RAT-A-TAT-TAT. RAT-A-TAT-TAT.* Over and over. Someone was impatient to get in.

'What's going on?' Charlie's dad cried, striding in from the kitchen, a bucket in his hand ready to milk the cows. He flung open the front door to find a short, blond-haired man in a neck brace staring at him. 'What's the meaning of this?'

'Where is he?' the man demanded. 'I want to see him.'

'What are you talking about? See who?' Charlie's mum said, joining his dad at the door. 'What's all the racket?'

'Jimmy,' the man replied. 'Where is he?'

'Might have guessed,' Charlie's dad muttered under his breath. He craned his neck. 'Jimmy!' he shouted up the stairs. 'Someone to see you!'

That's when Charlie realized something. Jimmy's bed was empty. The sleeping bag had been folded and placed neatly at the end of the camp bed. Charlie sat bolt upright. 'He's not here,' he shouted down.

'What?' Charlie's mum yelled back.

Charlie shot out of bed and raced downstairs. 'He's not here,' he repeated. 'His bed's been made.'

'Oh my God!' his mum cried. 'Something's happened to him. I just know it.'

'What do you want him for anyway?' Charlie's dad said, plonking down his bucket and peering at Neck Brace Man.

'He owes me money,' the man replied. He pointed to his neck brace. 'For this.'

Charlie's mum's eyebrows shot up. 'He wants to buy a neck brace off you?' she asked, surprised.

Neck Brace Man sighed. 'He *did* this to me.'

Charlie's mum clapped her hand over her mouth. 'Never! My Jimmy wouldn't hurt a fly.'

The man ran a hand through his hair and

avoided her eye. 'Well, all right, he didn't actually touch me,' he confessed, 'but he caused me to injure myself, let's just put it that way. He knows he did. So I want compensation from him. That's what.'

'How did you know he was here?' Charlie's dad asked.

Neck Brace Man coughed. 'I have my sources.'

'Very mysterious,' Uncle Martin piped up from the front garden, where he'd been raking the leaves. 'Maybe he's been abducted by aliens. Maybe he spontaneously combusted in the night.'

'Oh, don't be ridiculous, Martin,' Charlie's dad huffed. 'Most likely he's done a runner.'

'Oh, don't say that,' Charlie's mum cried, wringing her hands in anguish.

Charlie's dad shook his head ruefully. 'I hate to break it to you, love, but he's no angel. He'll have realized he's got himself into some pickle or other and taken off. Again.'

A sudden thought popped into Charlie's head. 'Wait!' he cried. 'No. No, he wouldn't . . .'

'What is it, love?' his mum asked.

Charlie burst through the front door, almost knocking over Neck Brace Man.

'Watch it!' the man shouted. He folded his arms. 'I can see it runs in the family.'

Charlie raced across the farmyard and round the back of the stables. He flew across the field and flung open the door to the barn.

He quickly counted one, two, three sheep. Where were the others? Where was Jessica Ennis-Hill?

And more importantly – WHERE WAS THE MOST IMPORTANT SHEEP?

Charlie raced out of the barn and looked back at everyone on the farmhouse steps. 'She's gone,' he cried, wiping his eyes with his pyjama sleeve. 'He's taken her.' He took a huge breath, a heavy sob working its way up his throat. 'Jimmy's stolen Alan Shearer.'

CHAPTER NINE

*C*harlie was inconsolable. His dad had told Neck Brace Man to get the heck off Argonaut Farm, but the man had said, 'I'm staying in rooms above the Golden Fleece pub in town and I'm not leaving until I get my compensation money,' and the pair of them had stood there arguing for ages.

His mum had enveloped Charlie in a hug and stroked his hair as he wept tears over the fact that he might never see his brother or Alan Shearer ever again. He didn't even know who he was more upset about losing.

Charlie told his mum that he wanted to be on his own for a while, and slunk off to the empty stables to get some peace and quiet. And it was while he was there, lamenting the loss of the lamb *and* his brother, that Uncle Martin sidled up to him.

'Pssssssst,' Uncle Martin hissed.

'What is it?' Charlie sniffed, not in the mood for Uncle Martin's games.

'I need to show you something. Come with me.'

Charlie wiped his eyes on his pyjama sleeve once more. 'I don't really feel like it, Uncle Martin,' he said, his voice croaky from all the sobbing.

'The sheep lives,' Uncle Martin whispered, somewhat mysteriously.

Charlie perked up at that. 'What?'

Uncle Martin grinned, propped his rake against the wall of the stables and beckoned for Charlie to follow him across the farmyard. They tiptoed their way towards the disused potting shed.

Uncle Martin looked about them to check the coast was clear before he opened the padlocked door. He tapped his nose. 'What you're about to see here,' he said, 'will surprise and amaze and befuddle you.' He grinned and flung open the shed door. 'Behold!'

Charlie peeked inside the shed and his jaw

dropped. He gazed up at Uncle Martin in wonder. 'How did you—?'

A broad grin broke across Uncle Martin's face. 'You're befuddled now, aren't you?'

Charlie nodded, for there, lying on a thick tartan blanket, with a crown that had been hastily fashioned from yesterday's newspaper on her head, and merrily chewing away on a bowl of grass was—

'Alan Shearer!' Charlie cried. He ran to the back of the shed, and fell to his knees beside her. 'You're here!' He stroked her on the head, and she bleated with pleasure.

'I thought she deserved better,' Uncle Martin explained. 'As soon as Mr Partridge said that she really was worth a fortune, I thought she should be living life in a manner that was fitting.'

Charlie looked at his uncle in confusion. 'What?'

'Well, she's famous, in't she?' Uncle Martin ploughed on. 'She's like the queen of the sheep. I'd have made her a throne, if I'd had the time last night, but I could only find that blanket. You'd never catch the *real* Queen living in a sheep pen with all the other regular sheep now, would you?'

Charlie didn't like to say that he highly doubted the Queen had been anywhere near a sheep pen in her life, but now wasn't the time to argue over such matters.

'I got the idea late last night, and put her in here so she could have her own space and her own bundle of straw and live like the royalty she is,' Uncle Martin finished. A frown passed across his face. 'You know, now the whole village knows we've got this famous sheep, we're gonna have all and sundry traipsing around trying to catch a glimpse of her. That's fine for selling my scones, but I don't like the thought of everyone gawping at her. She's too special.'

Charlie let out a huge sigh of relief. 'I thought Jimmy had stolen her. You know, gone back to his old ways.' He thought for a moment. 'But why is there another sheep missing?'

Uncle Martin grinned and tapped his nose again. 'That's the clever bit, see,' he said. 'I got one of the other sheep and I made her *look* like Alan Shearer, so no one would know the difference. Jessica Ennis-Hill, I think it was.'

'How did you make Jessica Ennis-Hill look like Alan Shearer?' Charlie asked.

'Black spray-paint,' Uncle Martin replied. 'There was some left over from doing the fencing panel the other day. I just copied the pattern of Alan Shearer's fleece onto Jessica Ennis-Hill's. Simple.'

Charlie got to his feet, trying to take everything in. 'So Jimmy's taken the wrong sheep?' he said after a moment. 'He *did* steal a sheep. He thought he was stealing Alan Shearer, but really he was stealing the sheep you'd made *look* like Alan Shearer? Jessica Ennis-Hill?'

'Jessica Ennis-Hill. Alan Shearer Two,' Uncle Martin said, nodding.

Well, that cleared everything up.

All of a sudden, they heard shouts coming from the farmhouse. Uncle Martin bustled Charlie out of the shed, padlocked the door closed, and the pair of them ran back round the stables to find Charlie's dad trapped in a headlock by a big brutish ex-WWE wrestler, while a thin wiry man and the man in the neck brace stood looking on.

'Let him go!' Charlie's mum screamed at the men.

'Not until we get our money,' the ex-wrestler (Brauns) the thin wiry man (Brains) and the man in the neck brace (who knew what his name was?) all yelled in unison.

Uncle Martin stepped forward. 'Is there a problem, Mick?' he said, drawing himself up to his full height.

Brains and Neck Brace Man shrank back a bit, but Brauns didn't take his arms from round Charlie's dad's head.

'No, no,' Charlie's dad hissed, his voice tight and strained, what with his neck being squeezed by a man whose arms were as thick as logs. 'I'm quite all right, Martin. Don't do anything rash. I'll fix this.'

Brains snapped his fingers and motioned for Neck Brace Man to head inside the farmhouse. 'Take whatever you can find that looks like it's worth a few bob,' he said.

Neck Brace Man ducked inside the farmhouse

and started rummaging around among the Rudges' possessions.

Uncle Martin raced after him. 'Oh no you don't!' he cried. 'Don't touch anything! Don't you dare even *look* at my limited-edition-mint-condition-never-been-opened Michael Bublé doll. IT'S STILL IN ITS ORIGINAL BOX!'

He bundled Neck Brace Man back out into the farmyard, empty handed.

'Dad?' Charlie asked. 'What's going on?'

Charlie's dad attempted to take a deep breath. 'I was just explaining to these men that they'd better get the heck off this farm as soon as possible, else there'll be hell to pay.'

Brains stepped forward. 'And we were just explaining to your dear dad here that none of us have the slightest intention of getting the heck off this farm until we get the money that is owed to us by one Jimmy Rudge.'

Charlie's dad tried to move his neck so he could breathe a little better. 'So I guess we're at an impasse,' he managed to squeeze out from his pressurized vocal cords.

'I thought we was at a farm?' Brauns said, confused.

Everyone stood there, looking at one another, no one quite sure what to do.

That's when they heard the bleat. A loud 'BAAAA' rang out around the farm.

And then, from round the corner, appeared Jimmy, carrying a sheep in his arms.

Jimmy stopped stock still as he took in the scene. 'What are you doing to my dad?' he cried. 'Let him go!'

'Jessica Ennis-Hill!' Charlie cried when he saw the sheep Jimmy was carrying in his arms, but no one paid the slightest bit of attention to him. That's what gave him the idea, actually.

Charlie's mum blew into a tissue. 'We thought you'd disappeared, love,' she said softly. 'Done a runner, like. Where have you been?'

Jimmy nodded to the sheep in his arms. 'I got up early this morning to muck out the sheep pen. And that's when I noticed that Alan Shearer was hobbling on her front hoof. So I took her to the vet's in the village, and he pulled out a thorn.'

Charlie's mum wiped her eyes. 'See?' she said to Charlie's dad. 'I told you he'd be good on a farm.'

Charlie's dad said, 'Hmph,' which may or may not have been an attempt to actually say something. His face was becoming red from being held in a headlock for so long, so it was a little difficult to tell.

'Good spot, Jimmy,' Uncle Martin piped up. 'I was so busy last night, I didn't notice anything wrong with Jessica—' He stopped abruptly as Charlie dug him in the ribs.

'With Alan Shearer,' Charlie prompted him. A look of confusion passed across Uncle Martin's face for a moment, but then he got it. 'Riiiiight.' He nodded, slowly. 'With Alan Shearer. That's right. When I saw her last night. With Alan Shearer. That sheep right there,' and he pointed at the sheep in Jimmy's arms. 'Alan Shearer.'

Jimmy raised an eyebrow, like he suspected Uncle Martin was having one of his funny moments.

'That's all very well,' Brains huffed. 'But I'd like to bring the conversation back to my original point. Where's my money?'

'*Our* money,' Neck Brace Man chipped in.

Jimmy sighed. 'I've already told you. You'll get it. I just need time.'

'We don't want to wait,' Brauns piped up.

Charlie's mum stepped forward. 'How much does he owe you?'

Jimmy shook his head. 'No, Mum. Don't.'

'But we might be able to help. How much?'

Brains smirked at her. 'Thousands. Seven thousand for us, to be precise,' and he motioned to himself and Brauns.

Charlie's mum gulped. So did Charlie's dad, but that may or may not have been an attempt to merely carry on breathing.

'Seven thousand pounds?' Charlie's mum whispered, looking as white as a sheet. 'How on earth did you . . . ?'

'Gambling, Mrs Rudge,' Brains chipped in. 'Poker. Blackjack. Scratch cards, you name it.'

Jimmy hung his head in shame. Even Alan Shearer Two (Jessica Ennis-Hill) bleated a little, but that may or may not have been because she could smell grass and it had been hours since she'd last eaten.

'Why doesn't that surprise me?' Charlie's dad muttered under his breath, but everyone heard him.

'And I want at least two thousand,' Neck Brace Man piped up. 'No. Three. Three thousand pounds.' He folded his arms.

'I didn't do anything to you,' Jimmy protested. 'You know it was an accident.'

'Your reckless running and barging past me made me fall over and crick my neck,' Neck Brace Man said. 'I have witnesses.'

'Who?'

'A vicar,' he stated. 'Whom, all right, I may or may not have bribed. But that's not the point. I'm a respectable citizen. I've climbed a mountain for charity. I help out at a care home once a month. I'm an IT manager, for heaven's sake. What with your criminal record, who do you think the police are likely to believe?'

Jimmy let out a puff of air. 'I just need time. That's all. Please.'

Brains grabbed Charlie's wrist and tapped his Newcastle United wristwatch. It was a Christmas present from his old friends at five-a-side football in Southend. He'd have felt a bit sad thinking about his friends back in Southend if he wasn't so busy worrying about the men trying to beat up his family. 'Hey!' he cried, wriggling out of Brains' grasp.

'Clock's ticking, Mr Rudge,' Brains sneered to Jimmy. 'We want our money by the end of the month, or there'll be hell to pay, all right.'

'I can't do that!' Jimmy cried.

Brains gave him a little smirk once more. 'No, no, that's fine. I'm sure your dad doesn't need *all* his fingers . . .'

Uncle Martin moved over to them, searching his pockets in vain for a rolling pin.

Charlie's mum started to sob uncontrollably.

'Stop!' Charlie cried. He couldn't bear it any more. 'All of you. Stop! Stop! You'll get your money, I promise!'

Everyone stopped in their tracks. Charlie spoke very quickly to get it all out before his courage deserted him.

'You'll get your money by the end of the month,' he explained, 'because we're rich. Bleeding, stinking rich. Well, we're gonna be, at any rate.'

Charlie's mum's mouth hung open in surprise. Brains stepped closer to him, as if to listen more attentively. 'Go on,' he said curiously.

'We're gonna have at least sixty thousand pounds,' Charlie continued, 'and so you'll get your seven thousand pounds, and he'll get his three thousand pounds, and there'll be enough left over for Dad to get his two tea rooms and a tractor and some horses. And a llama.'

'Enough with this flaming llama,' his mum hissed.

'How?' Brains asked, clearly intrigued.

'We're gonna set up a sheep auction,' Charlie stated matter-of-factly. 'We've got a Blackface ewe with a unique fleece. She's famous. She's really rare. She's worth a fortune. So we're gonna sell her and you'll get your money and then you can just push off.'

'No!' Charlie's mum cut in. 'You can't!'

'I can,' Charlie replied. 'We can. And we're gonna. We're gonna sell Alan Shearer.' And he pointed to the sheep that Jimmy was holding in his arms.

The sheep that was *not* Alan Shearer, but no one else knew that except Charlie and Uncle Martin.

Uncle Martin opened his mouth to say something, but Charlie nudged him in the ribs once more.

Brains, Brauns and Neck Brace Man all looked at one another in surprise.

Jimmy locked eyes with Charlie. 'I won't let you,' he whispered. 'Alan Shearer's yours.'

Charlie shrugged. 'As if I wouldn't do this for my brother. She's only a sheep.'

'You've changed your tune,' Charlie's dad hissed, but it sounded more like, 'Yveshngd yrchoon,' what with his head still being in a headlock.

'But what about the competition, Charlie?' Jimmy asked. 'That's at the end of the month, too. You need Alan Shearer to win.'

Charlie thought quickly. He knew that Alan Shearer was probably most definitely probably going to win the Best in Show round; Mr Partridge had practically said as much. But if he was meant to be selling Alan Shearer in an auction, even if the sheep they *really* sold was Jessica Ennis-Hill, he couldn't then wheel out the *real* Alan Shearer at the competition as if nothing had happened.

'You're right,' Charlie said. 'So there will be a condition of sale. We'll auction Alan Shearer on the Saturday, as long as the new owner lets me use her in the Young Farmer of the Year competition on the Sunday. They can take her away after that. What do you reckon?'

Charlie's dad nodded, as best he could with Brauns' meat cleavers for hands around his neck.

Brains stroked his chin, thinking it all over. 'Very well,' he mused. 'Very well. That's all anyone's been able to talk about in the Golden Fleece, this sheep of yours. I'm glad you've come to your senses.' He motioned to Brauns to let Charlie's dad go.

When Brauns released Mr Rudge's neck, the blood returned to his face almost immediately. He took lots of deep breaths. 'If you ever pull a stunt like that again—' he threatened, but Brauns didn't look too troubled.

Brains motioned to Brauns and Neck Brace Man, and the three of them turned and walked to the gate. 'We're sticking around,' Brains called back. 'To make sure you keep to your word and sell this sheep of yours. You've got till the end of the month. Two weeks. Like I said, none of us are leaving until we've got our money.'

Charlie shrugged his shoulders. 'If you want,' he said, and he watched their retreating backs as they sauntered across the fields.

Charlie's mum, dad, Jimmy and Uncle Martin looked at him in amazement.

'Are you sure?' Jimmy said after a moment. 'I just feel so − *bad* − making you do this.'

'You're not making me do this, it's my choice,' Charlie said matter-of-factly. 'Family's more important than sheep. I want to help.'

Charlie's mum hugged him. 'I'm so proud of you,' she said.

Charlie's dad slapped him on the back. 'Quite the big man,' he said, nodding in agreement, secretly pleased that Charlie had come to his senses and that his plans for expanding the farm − including buying that flaming llama − would be realized after all.

Uncle Martin tapped his nose and winked at Charlie, and Charlie motioned for him to keep quiet.

Jimmy plonked Alan Shearer Two (Jessica Ennis-Hill) on the ground, and reached over and ruffled Charlie's hair. 'Thanks, bro,' he whispered. 'You saved my bacon.'

And Alan Shearer Two (Jessica Ennis-Hill) bleated, 'BAΛΛΛΛΛΛΛ!' which didn't really add anything to the conversation, but was all anyone could expect of her, to be honest.

CHAPTER TEN

After the auction was announced, there was a distinct buzz around the village of Ovwick Rumble. More and more visitors turned up to the farm to catch a glimpse of the famous sheep and weigh up whether they could afford to bid for her or not.

Things had changed at school, too. One morning, as he crossed the three fields, climbed over the two stiles and hopped over the narrow stream to get there, Charlie could feel his ears burning. As he walked across the playground to the Portakabin, the six other children were huddled in a big circle, whispering to each other. Charlie caught the words 'thousands' and 'black-and-white stripes', and he guessed immediately they were talking about him. Or Alan Shearer, at any rate.

Charlie huffed, and carried on walking.

Just then, Saul broke out of the circle. 'Oi, Charlie,' he yelled across the playground. 'You think you're in with a chance?'

Charlie stopped and looked over at him. 'What are you talking about?' he asked.

'Young Farmers,' Saul continued. 'You think you can just swan into Ovwick Rumble and enter the competition in what, two weeks? What do you know about farming? About anything?'

Saul was right. Charlie didn't know much about farming, despite all the reading up on it he'd been doing. But he *did* know he had a secret weapon.

'Best in Show,' Charlie shot back at him, and he forced a little smile.

A short, dark-haired boy stepped forward from the others. 'Best in Show what?' he said.

'He means his sheep,' Saul sneered. He turned back to Charlie. 'But you're selling it.'

'Yes,' Charlie stated clearly, so that everyone could hear. 'But I'm not giving her to the new owners till after the competition. She'll be mine for the final round.' And he shot a pointed look at Saul.

The five other children started whispering to each other excitedly. 'He's got you there,' the dark-haired boy said to Saul. He pushed his hair out of his eyes and looked directly at Charlie. 'I'm Franco,' he said. 'We've not really spoken.'

Charlie could have said, 'Tell me about it.' He could have said, 'I know. I've been sitting on my own for the last few weeks. I've been ignored. I've been lonely. I've been wanting someone to have a kick-about with.' But he didn't. He cleared his throat, and nodded. The first person in Ovwick Rumble who'd been nice to him. Not counting Alan Shearer. 'Charlie Rudge,' Charlie said.

Saul arched an eyebrow. 'Final round,' he said. 'Really? How's your sheep-shearing?'

Charlie frowned. 'What?'

'Oh, nothing, nothing,' Saul laughed. He picked up his bag from the ground and slung it over his shoulder. 'Forget I even mentioned it.' He shot Charlie a half-taunting, half-pitying sneer, and headed inside the Portakabin.

Saul ignored him for the rest of the day, but Charlie wasn't fussed because he'd made a *little* bit of progress. He knew the names of the other children, of course – you couldn't sit in a Portakabin with just six others for a month and not find out their names – but this was the first time anyone had actually been nice to him. And all right, it wasn't as if he and Franco were friends, but still. He couldn't wait to get home and tell Alan Shearer.

But when Charlie left school that day and crossed the playground to the narrow stream, there, waiting for him on an old tree stump, was Jimmy.

'All right, bro?' Jimmy grinned as Charlie bounded over. 'How was school?'

Charlie shrugged. He wasn't really one for all that maths and science and learning malarkey. He'd rather be at home, helping out on the farm.

'Stick at it, mate,' Jimmy said. 'You don't want to end up like me.' He got to his feet and the two of them carried on walking downstream. Charlie looked down at the ground as he walked, his mind whirring with the competition. Something about what Saul had said niggled him.

'Penny for 'em,' Jimmy said, interrupting Charlie's thoughts.

Charlie kicked at the grass with the toe of his trainer. 'It's in less than two weeks,' he said.

Jimmy guessed what he was talking about. 'You nervous?'

Charlie shrugged again. 'Nervous. Under prepared.' He let out a huff. 'I can't do sheep-shearing.'

Jimmy threw his head back and laughed. 'What?' Charlie grumbled. 'I haven't had a chance to practise it. Stop laughing, this is important. Saul said . . . Jimmy, stop laughing!'

Jimmy nodded and leaned against a tree to get his breath back. 'I know, Charlie,' he said when he'd eventually calmed down. 'But there's no need to get so sad about it.'

Charlie gazed off into the distance. Neither of them said anything for a while.

Jimmy placed a hand on his shoulder. 'I'm sorry. I didn't realize this competition meant so much to you.'

'I want to win,' Charlie stated. 'I want to show everyone I can be a farmer.'

'You *are* a farmer,' Jimmy reasoned. 'You're doing a grand job on this farm.'

'That's not the point. I want to be a proper farmer. The *best* farmer.' Charlie looked down at his feet. 'I've never been the best anything before,' he said softly. 'And now we've got officially the best sheep in Scotland, I want to be officially the best young farmer.'

Jimmy frowned. 'Yeah, but not for ever.' He looked at Charlie guiltily. 'I mean, the auction. Alan Shearer may be there to help you win, but then she'll be going to her new home.'

Charlie looked Jimmy in the eye. Maybe he could tell him the truth. Maybe Jimmy would keep it a secret.

Jimmy gulped. 'You don't have to, you know,' he said. 'I know how much Alan Shearer means to you ...' He drifted off. Then he reached into his pocket and produced some notes and coins. He held them out to Charlie.

'Mrs Morrison gave it to me,' Jimmy explained. 'I fixed her lawnmower this morning. Go on, take it.'

'Why?' Charlie asked, surprised.

''Cos I'm gonna pay you back,' Jimmy returned. 'For Alan Shearer. Even if it takes the rest of my life to do it.'

A knot formed in Charlie's stomach. He couldn't take Jimmy's money. Not when he wasn't really selling Alan Shearer. Not when he was knowingly lying to everyone to get them all that cash.

No, Charlie reasoned. The fewer the number of people who knew what he was doing, the better. Best just stick to himself and Uncle Martin.

'There's no need,' Charlie replied, shaking his head. 'I'm happy to do it.'

Jimmy shot him a tight smile, then nodded across the field. 'Come on, then. Ice cream. My treat.'

Charlie looked at him curiously. He'd heard that many times before, and today he wasn't in the mood for running.

'I'm paying this time, I promise,' Jimmy said, as if reading Charlie's mind. 'Just don't tell Mum. She'll blame me for ruining your tea.'

He slung an arm round Charlie's shoulders. 'Tell you what,' he said. 'After ice cream, I'll give you a hand with sheep-shearing practice. Agreed?'

Charlie nodded. 'Agreed.'

It felt good to have his brother back. It felt good to be able to help him. Even if it did involve a teeny tiny lie about selling a sheep for more money than it's worth.

Still. It didn't matter how many times Charlie told himself that he was doing the right thing, the sinking, knotted feeling in his stomach didn't go away.

Maybe the ice cream would do it, he thought to himself. Only one way to find out.

CHAPTER ELEVEN

Charlie had to admit, it was nice sharing an ice cream with his brother knowing he wasn't going to have to leg it out of the shop afterwards. That was the one thing about Jimmy's previous trick – Charlie could never actually *enjoy* the ice cream or burgers or milkshakes or hot dogs that Jimmy ordered, because he knew there was a strong possibility he'd be seeing them all again when he was sick on the pavement after running on such a full stomach.

The only place to get ice cream in the village of Ovwick Rumble was Debbie & Dale's Dairy & Baked Goods Emporium, a twenty-minute walk from Ovwick Rumble Primary. Not that Jimmy minded, for he couldn't wait to see Eloise again. That was half the reason he'd suggested going.

Charlie pushed his empty bowl away from him, nicely stuffed after a double scoop of Let's Go Bananas and Coconuts. 'That didn't even touch the sides,' said Jimmy, smiling at him.

Charlie sat back in the booth, and leaned his head against the seat. He let out a contented sigh. 'What was it like?' he asked, after a moment.

Jimmy looked at him curiously. 'What was what like?'

'Living with Cousin Graham. In Cleethorpes.'

Jimmy snorted. 'Imagine living in a morgue.'

'Cousin Graham *does* live in a morgue,' Charlie stated.

'This is true,' Jimmy replied. 'But you know what I mean. It was boring.'

Charlie nodded. Cousin Graham was the son of Charlie's mum's older sister, and all his life, all he'd ever wanted was to be an undertaker. Charlie's mum said he'd always worn black, even as a baby, and he'd always had a fascination with the dead. So it was somewhat inevitable when he'd opened his own funeral director's in Cleethorpes. And apart from an unfortunate blip upon opening – when there had been a mix-up at the printer's, and Cousin Graham's shop sign had read WE DO FUNERALS! GRAHAM MARKBONE: DEAD EXCITED TO HELP! which didn't set the right sort of tone at all – he'd been busier than he'd ever dared dream.

'Mum and Dad sent me to live with Cousin Graham in the hope that he'd knock some sort of sense into me,' Jimmy said softly. 'And he did.' He rubbed his chin. 'Well, not Graham himself, exactly, but working at the funeral parlour.'

Charlie thought for a moment. 'I guess a funeral parlour isn't like an ice-cream parlour, right?' he said, looking around the Baked Goods Emporium.

Jimmy gave him a rueful smile. 'Being around all that death,' he said. 'All that sadness.' He pushed the last of his ice cream around his bowl, lost in thought. 'It made me realize that I wanted to live. Life's so precious, Charlie. And I wanted to spend it with the people I love.'

He looked at Charlie. 'So I came here.'

Charlie beamed back at him. And then he looked over towards the ice-cream counter, where Debbie, Eloise and Eloise's grandma, Madge, were serving customers. 'People you love?' he teased, nodding at Eloise. 'People you luuuuuuuuuuurrrve?'

Jimmy followed Charlie's gaze, and smiled when he saw Eloise.

At that moment, Eloise looked up from refilling the We're Minted! pot, and caught Jimmy's eye.

Unfortunately, so did Eloise's mum and grandma. Both ladies thought Jimmy was looking at them, and they both gave him a little wave of delight. Eloise's grandma licked her lips at Jimmy in appreciation, while Debbie winked seductively.

'Gross!' Charlie whispered.

Jimmy shuddered. 'I can't help it if I'm such a female magnet,' he whispered back. 'But that's ridiculous!'

Debbie plopped two large scoops of ice cream into two bowls and sauntered over to the table. 'All right, lads?' she asked, though she didn't so much as look at Charlie; her gaze was focused solely on Jimmy. 'These are on the house.'

She plonked the bowls down in front of them. 'Oh no,' Jimmy protested, holding up his hands, 'we couldn't possibly. We're stuffed.'

'Nonsense,' said Debbie, laughing. 'You're a growing lad.' And she stroked the muscles on Jimmy's arm.

Jimmy yanked his arm away so suddenly that he knocked the bowl of ice cream clean off the table. It smashed into pieces on the floor. 'ELOISE!' Debbie yelled. 'MOP!'

'Sorry,' Jimmy apologized as Eloise came scuttling out from behind the counter to clean up the mess. 'Here, let me.' He leaped up from the booth and dropped down to his knees to pick up the fragments of bowl.

His hands met Eloise's over the pool of melting Neapolitan Dynamite on the floor. Jimmy smiled at Eloise. She blushed madly, but the corners of her mouth twitched into a shy smile.

'It's my birthday soon!' Debbie declared from out of nowhere, breaking the romantic moment. 'How's about a kiss for the birthday girl?'

Jimmy straightened up. 'Errrrrr—' He looked from Charlie to the door and back again.

Here we go again, thought Charlie, and prepared to scarper. Just like old times.

'I've got a cold,' Jimmy said, holding his nose suddenly. 'Best not. Don't want you to catch anything.'

Debbie recoiled a bit. 'Oh, all right then,' she reasoned, though she couldn't help but look disappointed. 'Still. You'll join me for my birthday drinks, won't you? Last Thursday of the month at the Golden Fleece? I've booked a table from seven.'

Jimmy looked to Eloise. 'Are you going?' he whispered so Debbie couldn't hear. Eloise nodded.

'Sure,' Jimmy told Debbie. 'I'll be there.' He reached into his pocket and pulled out his wallet.

Debbie waved her hand. 'No, no. Like I said, it's on the house,' she trilled.

Jimmy motioned to Charlie. 'Thanks. That's very kind. We'll be off then.' He looked back to give Eloise one last smile. 'See you later,' he called.

'Not if I see you first,' Debbie and Madge said at the same time, both winking and waving at him.

As soon as they were round the corner, Charlie burst out laughing. 'Glad you find it funny,' Jimmy grumbled. He let out a puff of air. 'Right. Come on then. My side of the bargain. Sheep-shearing.'

He ruffled Charlie's hair and the pair of them walked home to Argonaut Farm.

There was something about sheep-shearing that Charlie just couldn't get the hang of. To be fair, only a month previously he'd been in Southend-on-Sea, a normal boy playing football and going down the arcades on the seafront. He'd never held a pair of shears before. He'd never held a *sheep* before. Holding the two at the same time was proving tricky.

Charlie had given Jimmy his *Farming Today* handbook and Jimmy read from the 'Instructions on Sheep-shearing' section. 'Right,' he said. 'Sit the sheep in first position and shear from the brisket to the belly.'

'Biscuit?' Charlie asked.

'Brisket,' Jimmy corrected him. 'Concentrate, Charlie.' He cleared his throat. 'First position is sitting the sheep up on her bum. Then you want to lay the sheep down, move from the belly wool to the legs and sort of unzip her fleece, like you're unzipping a jumper. Then stand her up and finish with shearing the tail and hind legs. All right?'

Jimmy grabbed the only sheep they'd managed to coerce into being there – David Beckham. They'd originally tried for Muhammad Ali, only to discover that he had a nervous disposition. Every time Charlie moved the shears in Muhammad Ali's direction, he would bleat maniacally. He'd also run off. And no amount of calling, 'Wheeet-wheeeo. Wheeet-wheeeo. Come by. Come by,' would persuade Bessie to round him up again. But David Beckham was the most docile of all the sheep, and had gamely followed them outside to the yard when they'd waved a bowl of grass under his nose. He had no idea of the fate that lay in store for him.

'Sounds simple enough, doesn't it?' Jimmy said, grinning.

Charlie tried propping David Beckham up so he was sitting on his backside. He bit his lip in concentration. This wasn't simple at all.

David Beckham waddled about for a minute, but then eventually slumped down on his bottom. Charlie held him in place, while Jimmy picked up the shears and passed them over. They smelled of motor oil and grease.

David Beckham let out a small bleat, almost like a whimper, as the shears started down his belly. 'I don't like getting my hair cut,' Charlie stated. 'I know how they feel.'

It was rather wobbly going at first, and Charlie's hand quickly grew heavy from the shears. 'That's it,' Jimmy soothed. 'Just keep calm. Breathe nice and slow. You've got it.'

David Beckham bleated again but he didn't look like he minded too much. 'Now try the unzipping the fleece bit,' Jimmy said.

Charlie grabbed hold of David Beckham's belly and tried to lift him onto his legs, but his hands were tired and he lost his balance, and as David Beckham scrambled to his feet, Charlie's grasp on the shears loosened and they ran away with themselves, zigzagging their way across the fleece.

'That's not what I meant by unzipping the fleece, Charlie,' Jimmy laughed.

Tufts of wool flew through the air as a large bald patch appeared down David Beckham's right-hand side. Sweeney Todd had nothing on Charlie's barbering skills, clearly.

The shears fell to the ground, still twitching and buzzing feverishly. David Beckham ran off at his first chance, bleating wearily as he shot across the yard, back to the safety of the barn.

Charlie let out a puff of air. 'I'm never gonna do it,' he moaned. 'I'm not gonna win the competition by giving a sheep a short back and sides, am I?'

Jimmy had learned his lesson from last time and managed to hold in his laughter. 'You'll get there, mate,' he said sincerely. 'I know you will. We've got twelve days till the competition. Plenty of time to practise.' He nodded towards the barn. 'We'll try shearing his other half later. What's next on the list?'

He looked down at the notes Charlie had made inside the *Farming Today* handbook. Next on the list was 'Best in Show' but Jimmy didn't think it wise to mention that. Not when Charlie was having to sell the best Best in Show contender in Scotland to help him out. 'Driving a tractor round an obstacle course,' Jimmy said. 'How are we going to practise that?'

Charlie shrugged. He kicked at a small stone on the ground. 'Dunno,' he said glumly.

'Cheer up, Charlie,' Jimmy said. 'I promise you I'm going to help you with this. You'll do it, I swear.'

He grinned at Charlie and something about his smile made Charlie grin right back at him, despite how utterly fed up he was feeling.

'Woof! Woof, woof!'

At that moment, Bessie bounded out of the door of the farmhouse and ran over to them. She stopped at Charlie's feet, wagging her tail in delight.

Jimmy raised an eyebrow. 'We could try the "Best Sheepdog at Rounding Up Sheep" round?'

Charlie let out another sigh. He loved Bessie, she was a faithful dog – but a champion sheepdog she was not.

'Just give it a try,' Jimmy soothed.

Charlie patted down his jeans and pulled out his whistle from his back pocket. He thought for a moment. Which command should he go for?

'Whee-whee-wheeet,' meant 'Come here.' He blew three times into his whistle.

Bessie sat there, looking up at him, wagging her tail.

Charlie tried once more. 'Whee-whee.' Two short whistles meant 'Walk up.'

Bessie still sat there, still looking up at him, still wagging her tail. Charlie was beginning to see a pattern emerging. 'It's not working,' he moaned to Jimmy.

Jimmy nodded. He slapped his thigh. 'Come on, girl,' he called to Bessie. 'Come here. Come on, girl.'

Bessie didn't move. 'Can you get deaf dogs?' Charlie asked Jimmy. He could feel the Young Farmer's crown slipping away from him, minute by minute.

'Bessie!' Jimmy called again. 'Here are the sheep.' He pointed to the barn. 'And your job is to round them up. Come on, girl.'

'Please,' Charlie added. 'Come on, Bess.'

Bessie whumped her tail on the ground and cocked her head to one side, as if mulling over Charlie's pleas.

And then, as if by magic, she trotted over to the barn and peered inside.

'Hooray!' Charlie yelled.

'Progress!' Jimmy cried.

Charlie put the whistle to his lips once more. 'Who-Hee-Who.' Three short blows. 'Who-Hee-Who.'

And then, by some sort of miracle – or more likely because Bessie just so happened to turn her head at the exact moment that Charlie whistled the command for 'Look back', Bessie looked back at him. She actually looked back at him. This *was* progress!

Jimmy patted Charlie on the back. 'There you go,' he laughed. 'What did I tell you? You'll be champion before you know it.'

'Practice makes perfect,' a voice piped up from the farmhouse steps behind them.

Charlie and Jimmy turned to see their dad standing in the doorframe, his arms folded, a reluctant smile on his face. 'Well done, Charlie, lad.'

Charlie frowned. 'We're not there just yet,' he said, gesturing to Bessie. 'But Jimmy helped, too.'

Charlie's dad nodded. 'So he did,' he replied. 'So he did.'

Charlie's mum joined Charlie's dad on the

doorstep, draping her arm round his shoulders. 'Look at this,' she said, a giant beam on her face. 'My boys, all together again. I couldn't be happier.' She kissed her husband on the cheek. 'I told you he'd be good on a farm.'

Charlie's dad looked around the farmyard. Fresh bundles of hay were neatly stacked by the empty horse stables. The wonky leg of the chicken coop had been fixed. The pigs' trough was full of clean water. *And* the creaky gate in the front garden had been oiled and re-hung. All of which was Jimmy's handiwork, his dad couldn't deny it.

He nodded. 'You've been busy, Jimmy,' he said. 'Well done.'

Jimmy blushed, but he couldn't hide his delight at the praise.

Uncle Martin walked over to them from the tea room, munching on a slice of Battenburg. 'Another cracking day for sales,' he said between bites. 'And I am *this* close to winning a signed 2006 Michael Bublé calendar on eBay.'

'I've been researching Brand Identity on the internet so we can have signs run up,' Charlie's mum stated. '*Argonaut Farm*,' she said, waving her hand in the air dramatically, '*Home of the Famous Sheep with the Fleece*.'

Charlie's dad nodded. 'I've been researching what you need to feed a llama.'

Everyone laughed at that.

Charlie looked at his mum, dad and Uncle Martin, all pleased as punch in the doorway. *Life* is *precious*, he thought to himself, echoing Jimmy's words from earlier. *You* should *spend it with the people you love*.

He beamed from ear to ear as he thought how nice it was to have his brother back, to live on a farm with the family and animals he loved, even if he had just shorn a bald patch on one of his sheep and had the doziest sheepdog in the world. Mostly he thought how nice it was not to have to run away from a café and risk seeing the contents of his stomach on the street again.

Life was precious indeed.

CHAPTER TWELVE

It was a sunny Sunday morning in late May, unusually sunny for Ovwick Rumble, and for Scotland in general, and Charlie's mum was taking the opportunity to sunbathe. She was sitting in one of the rusty chairs in the farmyard in her pink bikini, leafing through a glossy magazine. Charlie's dad was taking a well-earned rest from mucking out the pigs in the barn and sat on the farmhouse steps, slurping a mug of tea.

With exactly one week until the competition, Charlie had to up his preparations. He snuck past his parents and made his way to the disused potting shed at the back of the empty stables. The door was slightly ajar when Charlie got there, and he poked his head in to see Uncle Martin sweeping the floor all round Alan Shearer's tartan-blanket-clad bed. When he'd finished, he gave a small curtsy to Alan Shearer, as if she really was the Queen, and propped the broom up against the wall.

Charlie stepped into the shed and Uncle Martin spun round like a shot. He breathed a sigh of relief when he saw it was only Charlie. 'I nearly jumped out of my skin!' he cried. He gestured to the shed door. 'Be careful with the door, it's a bit dodgy. It keeps swinging open of its own accord. It's on my list of things to do.'

Charlie walked over to Alan Shearer and smoothed her back. 'She's so soft,' he exclaimed in amazement. 'Her fleece is like stroking . . . well, something that's really soft. Like cotton wool. Or candyfloss. It's like stroking candyfloss.'

Uncle Martin beamed. He reached over to a shelf on the far side of the shed and took down a bottle from it. '*Strengthening, restorative shampoo, with natural oils and added volumizer and anti-breakage properties for hair that's truly silky smooth,*' he said like he was in an advert for L'Oréal. 'It's your mum's. I've been shampooing her twice a day.' He thought for a moment. 'Alan Shearer, obviously. Not your mum.'

Charlie beamed. He unzipped his jacket and pulled out a small rectangular cloth bag from inside. From that, he took out a set of heated rollers. 'I nicked them from Mum's dressing table,' he whispered. 'Thought we could give Alan Shearer's fleece a bit of bounce. That's what Mum's always saying her hair needs. They're thermo-ceramic, apparently, whatever that is.'

Uncle Martin nodded. 'Great minds think the same thing sometimes,' he said, wisely. Well, wisely for him.

Charlie took a couple of rollers out of the bag. 'Yeowch!' he cried, his finger sizzling on the still-warm rollers. 'They're hot!'

Uncle Martin reached for a roller at the exact same time as Charlie kneeled down next to Alan Shearer, and somehow he ended up butting his head against Charlie's hand.

He clapped his hand to his head. 'My eye!' he cried.

Charlie sniffed, and the distinct smell of burning filled the shed.

Uncle Martin released his hand from his forehead and Charlie almost burst out laughing. Half his eyebrow above his right eye had singed, ever so slightly. A few hairs had come away in his hand, the pink and raw skin underneath peeking through.

Charlie giggled, and after a moment, Uncle Martin joined in, too. Then he reached up to a shelf on the wall of the shed and took down a large paddled hairbrush. 'Do you want to do the honours?' he said, handing it to Charlie.

Charlie brushed Alan Shearer's fleece gently. It had grown so much in the past few weeks, at least a few centimetres. He knew he was probably biased, but it really *was* the softest, loveliest, fluffiest fleece in the land.

'How are you feeling?' Uncle Martin asked. 'About the competition?'

Charlie was nervous, in all honesty. On top of that, he was feeling guilty. Not just because he was lying to everyone – his family, the village of Ovwick Rumble, the potential buyers, everyone who had come to Argonaut Farm and paid their one pound entry fee to see their famous sheep, not realizing it was a run-of-the-mill ewe with spray-painted markings.

Charlie was also feeling guilty about the fact that he hadn't seen Alan Shearer in days. He'd been so busy hanging out with Jimmy, enjoying having his brother back, practising for the competition, that he hadn't been spending as much time with her as he normally did. Considering she was his best friend.

Charlie shrugged and carried on brushing. 'All right, I guess,' he said. 'It's not really the competition I'm worried about.'

Uncle Martin nodded. 'I know how you feel.' He shot Charlie a tight smile. 'It'll be fine,' he said. 'I'm sure it will be.'

Uncle Martin watched Alan Shearer chew her hay for a moment, and then he got to his feet. 'Right,' he said. 'I'll leave you to it. Going to make the most of the sunshine.'

Charlie smiled as Uncle Martin left the shed, and carried on brushing Alan Shearer. She bleated happily as the hairbrush ran over her fleece.

'You haven't got a care in the world, have you?' Charlie laughed. 'Man, it's easy being a sheep.

You couldn't care less that none of the other sheep talk to you. You couldn't care less that you might be found out lying and cheating and faking things to get money to pay off the men your brother owes money to. You couldn't care less that you're probably never going to see your old friends again.'

A sudden thought popped into his mind. 'Hey!' he cried. He got to his feet and looked out of the shed window. If he squinted, he could just about make out his mum and dad sitting in the farmyard. And Uncle Martin, who had joined Charlie's mum in sunbathing, and was sitting on the other rusty chair in his bright purple Speedos. And there, coming back up the dirt track having taken Bessie for a walk, was Jimmy.

With all the farming and competition practice he'd been doing, not to mention all the faking and grooming sheep, he'd completely forgotten about something. He gave Alan Shearer a kiss on her head, put the hairbrush back on the shelf, and raced out of the shed. 'See ya, Alan!' he yelled as he flew round the stables and across the farmyard.

He came to a stop in front of his family. 'Me,

you,' Charlie panted, trying to get his breath back, and pointing to Jimmy, 'Mum, Dad, Uncle Martin. Our five-a-side football team! We've not played since you came back!'

Charlie's mum rolled her eyes. 'You don't want me to play, love,' she said. 'You know I'm hopeless at footie.' She patted her hair. Tried to act casual. 'You know, me and your dad, we were thinking you could maybe ask your friends round to play. You know, from school? One of your friends from school could come round and play footie? Weren't we, Mick? Mick!' She nudged Charlie's dad in the ribs and he spluttered out a mouthful of tea.

'Oh, what? Yes!' he blustered. 'It's all very well us being a five-a-side team, but we'll need people to play against. Invite all your friends over.'

Charlie coolly ignored them. 'I'll go and change into my Magpies kit,' he said. He couldn't face telling them that he didn't have anyone to ask from school. That only one boy, Franco, had bothered to be nice to him once during the whole time he'd been there. Besides, he had too much on his mind with the competition and auction to worry about anything else. 'It'll be just like old times. Like in Southend.'

Charlie's dad opened his mouth to say something, but Jimmy shot him a look. 'There'll be plenty of time for that later,' he said, and bent down to detach the lead from Bessie's collar. 'For now, we need to concentrate on the competition. It's in just seven days!'

Charlie's mum clapped her hands together. 'Ooh, how are you getting on, love?' she said. 'You've been training so hard for it. Why don't you show us what you can do?'

It was true – over the last few days, Charlie had practised for the Young Farmer of the Year competition with all the dedication and drive of a champion boxer preparing for his next fight. He was Joe Frazier vs Muhammad Ali (not the sheep). Lennox Lewis vs Frank Bruno. Rocky versus Apollo Creed. (Bad example. Rocky didn't win that one.)

'Drop and give me twenty!' Jimmy yelled at Charlie, and Charlie instinctively flung himself to the ground and started doing push-ups. His arms were wobbly, and he collapsed on the grass after his fifth attempt.

'Why am I doing this?' he moaned.

'Just wait there,' Jimmy said, and he dashed into the farmhouse. Moments later, he reappeared brandishing the *Farming Today* manual and turned to the page of sheep-shearing instructions.

'Because it says here,' Jimmy said, reading from the page, 'that sheep-shearing requires skill, patience, stamina and strength. Only attempt to shear a sheep if you can comfortably bench-press 120 pounds.'

Charlie thought for a moment. 'I don't know what bench-press 120 pounds means,' he said, 'but I know that Alan Shearer's worth at least sixty thousand pounds, so I'll probably be all right.'

Everyone burst out laughing at that, though Charlie didn't know why.

'I've been thinking,' his mum mused. 'I know you want to spruce this place up, but we could use some of the money from the auction to go on holiday. That'd be nice, wouldn't it? Two weeks in Marbella? That'd do me. Oh, go on, Mick. We've not had a decent holiday in ages.' She looked over her arms and legs. 'I'm dying for a proper tan.'

Charlie's dad guzzled his tea. 'Let's not get carried away,' he said. 'I don't know how much a llama costs yet.' He frowned at Charlie. 'And talking of sheep, don't forget David Beckham. He's been wandering around with half a fleece for the last week.' He drained the last of his tea. 'Tell you what, I'll give you a hand with the sheep-shearing. It's something I need a little practice in myself.'

Jimmy smiled at him. 'I can help, too,' he said. 'It's all in here.' He nodded to the manual.

Charlie's dad raised his mug. 'Right you are, lad,' he said. 'That'd be grand.' He turned to Charlie. 'Why don't you go and fetch David Beckham? Or any of them. They could all do with a shear, probably. Go and fetch Jessica Ennis-Hill.'

'NO!' Charlie blurted out before he could help himself. Jessica Ennis-Hill was currently pretending to be Alan Shearer.

His dad looked startled.

'She's, uh, she's having a lie down,' Charlie stuttered, trying to think on his feet. 'I've just given them all a feed, and they're a bit tired, I think. It's the sun and the hot weather, probably. Made them all a bit sleepy, I think.'

Charlie's dad narrowed his eyes, but he nodded, slowly. 'Very well,' he said. 'You're in charge. As long as they're fed and watered, that's all that matters.'

'Why don't we try the tractor round?' Jimmy piped up.

'Because we haven't got a tractor,' Charlie replied.

'We could create an obstacle course anyway,' Jimmy said. 'Including a hoop of fire. I'll time you while you run down to the gate, go round it twice, over to the stables, round by the potting shed—'

'NOOOOOOOOOOOOOOOOOOOO!' Uncle Martin interjected. 'NOT THE POTTING SHED! NOOOOOOOOOOOOOOOOOOO!'

Everyone turned to look at him.

'So that's a no, then?' Jimmy asked.

Only Charlie knew why Uncle Martin was getting so worked up.

'It's got something of mine in there,' Uncle Martin said slowly, desperately trying to think of an excuse. 'Something I've been working on. It's – um – ummmmm—'

'Your Michael Bublé VIP Experience?' Charlie blurted. 'That's what it is. The complete tour. There's a waxwork model of him, a fascinating history of his childhood and then a two-hour song-for-song re-enactment of his 2012 sell-out tour at the O2. Right? All for £9.99, coming soon. Right?'

Charlie's mum, dad and Jimmy looked more baffled than ever. Uncle Martin nodded. 'Right. It'll be a hit. More popular than the tea room. You mark my words.'

Charlie's dad narrowed his eyes at Martin, like he suspected he was up to something. 'What happened to your eyebrow?' he asked, peering at the singed hair on Uncle Martin's face.

Uncle Martin clapped his hand to his forehead. 'Beauty disaster,' he said, and he buried his head in Mum's glossy magazine like it was the most fascinating thing he'd ever read.

'Talking of beauty,' Charlie's mum piped up.

'Has anyone seen my shampoo? I only bought a new bottle last week and now it's nowhere to be seen.'

Charlie and Uncle Martin exchanged a look and Charlie had to bite down on his lip to stop himself laughing.

Just seven more days, he thought to himself. Just seven more days and this madness would be over. In six days, the auction would be done, the money men paid off and Jessica Ennis-Hill given away to a new home pretending to be Alan Shearer. In seven days, Charlie would be the proud owner of the Young Farmer of the Year crown.

He just had to make sure everything went smoothly till then. Just seven more days.

CHAPTER THIRTEEN

Two days before the auction, a sudden thought popped into Charlie's mind. Alan Shearer was famous for her fleece, it was true. Not just her markings, but Mr Partridge had said the *quality* of the wool, the softness, the texture, the character, all combined to make her rare.

Whoever successfully bid for the sheep would be expecting a soft, beautiful fleece. Which Jessica Ennis-Hill definitely did *not* have. Why would she? She was just a regular sheep. Nothing special about her.

So after dinner, Charlie snuck across the farm to the barn, grabbed an empty bucket from the stables and filled it with water from the outside tap. He hauled open the barn door and ducked into the sheep pen.

Alan Shearer Two (Jessica Ennis-Hill) was sound

asleep on a bed of hay, no tartan blanket or crown fashioned from old newspaper for her. Charlie knelt down beside her, took a bottle of his mum's volumizing shampoo out of his jacket, and started rubbing the shampoo and water into Alan Shearer Two (Jessica Ennis-Hill)'s fleece. He made sure to work round the markings, so that the black spray-paint wouldn't come off.

'Charlie?' Uncle Martin called. Charlie looked up to see him standing in the doorway. 'What are you up to?'

Charlie nodded to Alan Shearer Two (Jessica Ennis-Hill). 'She'll never be as soft as the real thing,' he said, 'but hopefully no one will notice.'

Uncle Martin grinned and scooted into the barn. 'I didn't even think of that!' he whispered. 'You're a criminal mastermind!'

He stepped into the sheep pen and knelt down beside Charlie, watching him lather Alan Shearer Two (Jessica Ennis-Hill)'s fleece with the shampoo. Bubbles formed on top of bubbles, and soon it was pretty hard to see the sheep underneath it all.

After a moment, Charlie cleared his throat.

'Do you miss Southend?' he said in a small voice. 'Sometimes?'

Uncle Martin looked at him. 'What's brought this on?'

'I was just thinking,' he said. 'I miss my friends sometimes. I miss playing footie with them, and talking about Newcastle United. You know Dad doesn't like me to.'

'Oh, I wouldn't pay too much attention to that,' Uncle Martin replied. 'Your dad's not *really* angry that you've always supported Newcastle instead of Southend, he just doesn't understand it. None of us do, I suppose. But each to their own.' He thought for a moment. 'You know, I do and I don't miss it,' he went on. 'I miss my book-club pals. I miss my morris-dancing buddies. I miss my knitting circle.' He shrugged. 'But I love it up here. I love the tea room. I love the animals. I can knit anywhere. I'm sure I can find *someone* in Scotland who likes reading and dancing the morris.'

Charlie nodded. 'Yeah. I suppose. It's just . . . what Mum said the other day. About inviting friends over to play. I've not really . . . I mean, there's that

Saul Hoskins, but you saw what he's like. I don't really know anyone . . .' His voice trailed off.

Uncle Martin took a rag out of his trouser pocket and dipped it in the bucket of water. He started rinsing the shampoo off Alan Shearer Two (Jessica Ennis-Hill)'s fleece, pretending all the while that he couldn't see the tears in Charlie's eyes.

After a moment, Charlie gulped. 'I don't want Jimmy to go away again, either.'

Uncle Martin put down the rag and put a hand on Charlie's shoulder. 'It's like your mum says. Ovwick Rumble, this farm, it's a fresh start for all of us.' He smiled at him. 'I have a feeling everything's going to work out, Charlie. You'll see.'

And that's when they heard the scream from the farmhouse.

'AAAAAAAAAAAAAARRRRGGGHHHH!'

It was a high-pitched scream, short and urgent. It sounded like a woman being strangled.

'Here we go again,' Uncle Martin sighed. 'MICK!'

Charlie wiped the last of the shampoo suds off Alan Shearer Two (Jessica Ennis-Hill)'s fleece, picked up the bucket of water, and the two of them crept out of the barn, closed it behind them, and made their way towards the farmhouse.

As they got closer, Charlie's dad's voice drifted across the farmyard. 'OVER MY DEAD BODY!!!!!!'

'Come on, Mick,' Charlie's mum soothed. 'It's just a couple of drinks.'

Charlie's dad folded his arms and looked Jimmy squarely in the eye. 'That's what I'm worried about.'

Jimmy let out a puff of air. 'For goodness' sake, Dad,' he said. 'I've told you. I've learned my lesson. I'm not gonna do anything silly like steal a car and drive off down the seafront again.' He snorted. 'It's a hell of a drive to Southend, for one thing.'

'Don't get smart with me,' Charlie's dad warned. 'This isn't a laughing matter.'

Charlie and Uncle Martin bustled into the kitchen, trying to act like they hadn't just been up to something.

'What's going on?' Charlie asked.

'I was just telling Dad I've been asked out for drinks tonight,' Jimmy replied. 'With Eloise.'

Charlie's eyebrows shot up, and Jimmy blushed. 'I mean, for her mum's birthday drinks. Eloise will be there, obviously.'

Charlie nodded, remembering the awkward invitation. He reached for his *Farming Today* book on the sideboard, scraped back a chair and plonked himself down at the kitchen table. He turned to the page with the heading 'Finding a Needle in a Haystack' and tried to ignore the argument flying over his head.

'He deserves a night off,' Charlie's mum chipped in. 'He's worked so hard these past few weeks. Everyone can see that he's changed. You know it, Mick.'

She placed a comforting hand on Charlie's dad's arm. 'It'd do him good to make some friends in the village. Give him a break, love.'

Charlie's dad frowned, mulling this over. 'Fine,' he grumbled eventually. 'Just don't have more than one pint. Don't get drunk. And no gambling, all right? No bets. Don't—'

'You're a fine one to talk,' Charlie's mum said under her breath, but everyone heard her.

Charlie's dad stared at her. 'What's that supposed to mean?'

'It means the apple never falls far from the tree, Mick,' she replied. 'That's what.'

Uncle Martin frowned. 'We don't have an apple tree,' he piped up, but everyone ignored him.

Charlie cleared his throat. 'I think he should go,' he said, softly. 'He's been brilliant these past few weeks, helping me with the competition and everything. I don't feel half as nervous about Sunday as I would have done without him.' And, Charlie reasoned, though he didn't say it out loud, if Jimmy went to the pub and found friends in Ovwick Rumble, and maybe asked Eloise to be his girlfriend, well, he'd be more likely to stick around then, wouldn't he?

Charlie's dad sighed and eased himself into an armchair. 'Don't do anything foolish,' he said softly. 'That's all. Just watch yourself.'

Jimmy nodded. 'I will,' he said, making a cross in front of his heart. 'I swear. Thanks, Dad.'

He gave his mum a peck on the cheek. 'Thanks, Mum. See you later.'

He squeezed Charlie's shoulder. 'Night, mate,' he said, 'Night, Uncle Martin,' and he breezed out of the door.

Charlie's mum bustled round the stove, boiling the kettle. Charlie's dad switched on the TV and flicked through the channels until he came to the football. Uncle Martin took his knitting out of the fridge and sat down to work on his design of Michael Bublé's face. Charlie continued to read his book.

Normality was restored. All was peaceful in the Rudge household.

Until it wasn't, precisely five hours later, when Jimmy came crashing back into the front room, a hooting tawny owl strapped to his arm.

But we'll get to that in a bit.

CHAPTER FOURTEEN

The Golden Fleece was the only pub in the village, and also the only place where out-of-towners could stay. Three of its four guest rooms were currently occupied by Brains, Brauns and Neck Brace Man. The fourth room was currently occupied by a small Russian lady who has nothing to do with this story. She was, in fact, an assassin preparing for her mission to kill the Russian Ambassador, but that's a whole different kettle of fish.

Brains and Brauns had been staying at the Golden Fleece for the last two weeks since they'd threatened Charlie's dad. They'd meant what they said – they were going nowhere without their money. They hadn't really had much to do during that time, and had decided to treat their stay as a sort of holiday.

They very rarely got to take a break in their line of work. Sure, they often travelled, because the people who owed them money lived all over the UK. But they rarely had a day off from all the threatening and head-squashing, and it was such *tiring* work.

For the past two weeks, Brains and Brauns had fallen into a rather pleasant routine. They'd spend the day doing crossword puzzles (Brains) and squat thrusts (Brauns), then take a nice stroll around the village of Ovwick Rumble, visiting, in turn, the Ovwick Rumble Keyring Museum, the Ovwick Rumble Museum of Banisters, and the Ovwick Rumble Doorknob Museum (which, disappointingly, was just somebody's front room with a collection of six brass doorknobs), before returning to the Golden Fleece for a nice light dinner of calamari and chips, washed down with a pint of ale.

That evening, Brains and Brauns had seated themselves in their usual spot, a booth at the back of the pub. The Golden Fleece was an old pub, dating from the seventeenth century, with wood-panelled walls, low beams, and dark and secret corners, and no one paid the slightest attention to them. This was the most relaxed either of them had felt in years. Brains had taken out his *Sudokus That Even Einstein Would Find Hard Going* book and was working away at it, while Brauns had taken out a nail file and hand lotion and was sculpting his cuticles and manicuring his nails. Just because his hands were normally around somebody's neck didn't mean that he shouldn't take care of them.

From where they were sitting, Brains and Brauns could see Debbie from Debbie & Dale's Dairy & Baked Goods Emporium, Madge, Eloise, and a few other people from Ovwick Rumble who were there to celebrate Debbie's birthday. The table they were sitting round had cards, presents and a half-eaten cake on it, and different-coloured balloons were tied with string to the backs of the chairs, all, worryingly, featuring Michael Bublé's face. Hovering awkwardly around the table, not quite meeting Eloise's eye, was Jimmy.

Brains kept looking up from his sudoku and over to Jimmy, taking in the scene. He was finding it difficult to concentrate on his puzzle, knowing Jimmy was just over the way. For every time Brains looked at Jimmy, his face grew hot and his relaxed state slowly evaporated. One thought kept churning over and over in his mind. *WHY SHOULD HE GET IT ALL?*

Brains let out a puff of air and placed his sudoku book on the table.

'Too much for you, is it?' Brauns said, looking up from filing his nails.

Brains snorted in disgust. 'Hardly,' he muttered. 'I just have other things on my mind.'

Brauns nodded. 'Like, what museum are we going to tomorrow?' he said. 'I've been wondering that, too. The Ovwick Rumble Museum of Cat Hair is meant to be quite good.' He grinned at Brains. 'Who knew one little village would have so many museums?'

Brains' face softened at that, and he looked at Brauns thoughtfully. 'What would you do if you had a lot of money, Brauns?' he enquired. 'A *lot* of money?'

'Like, twenty quid?' Brauns asked. 'Probably spend it on sweets.'

Brains let out another sigh. 'No,' he said slowly, 'not twenty pounds.' He tried another tack. 'What would you love to do more than anything in this world?' He gazed wistfully into the distance. 'You must have dreams, Brauns? You must want more from life than beating people up for a few quid here and there.'

Brauns placed his nail file on the table and mulled it over. This was the deepest conversation he'd ever had with anyone, let alone Brains, whom he'd known for seven years now, ever since Brains had hired him to put an old lady in a headlock for not giving him the money he was after. It was only later that Brauns had found out that the old lady was, in fact, Brains' mum.

'I'd like my own pub,' Brauns replied after a moment.

Brains narrowed his eyes at him. 'Are you just saying that because we're currently sitting in a pub and you couldn't think of anything else to say? If we were currently sitting in a launderette, would you say you'd like your own set of washing machines and tumble dryers?'

Brauns shook his head. 'No,' he replied firmly. 'I've always wanted to have my own pub. Look at him.'

He nodded to the landlord, standing behind the bar, pulling a pint of beer and laughing with a customer. 'He looks like he's having a whale of a time. You'd get to chat to people and drink beer and eat pork scratchings and crisps and those nobbly nuts and play darts and sing karaoke and lift barrels of ale and eat calamari and chips and sit on barstools all day long.'

He looked slyly at Brains. 'And I've been thinking, we could run it together. You and me.'

Brains raised an eyebrow at him.

'We wouldn't even have to buy any signs, either,' Brauns ploughed on, and he picked up the little drinks menu that was resting on the table. 'Look.' The menu had THE GOLDEN FLEECE PUBLIC HOUSE AND B&B written at the top of it. 'It's already got our names on. B and B. That's us! Brains and Brauns.'

Brains looked at Brauns curiously, almost as if he was seeing him in a totally new light. 'I had no idea you wanted to be a publican,' he said softly. Who knew Brauns had such dreams?

Brauns frowned. 'I don't want to be a pelican,' he replied. 'I want to run a pub.'

Brains smiled at that, and after a moment

Brauns grinned right back at him. This was the best conversation they'd *ever* had.

Then a dark shadow passed across Brains' face. He shook his head. 'It's not enough,' he sighed. 'The money we're owed from Jimmy Rudge. It won't be enough for you to buy a pub, I'm afraid. I'm no expert, but I don't think you can buy a pub for seven thousand pounds. Not in this day and age.'

Brauns looked downcast. He'd allowed himself to reveal his deepest, darkest, most secret wish and had dared to dream it might possibly happen.

Brains gazed intently at Brauns. 'Not unless . . .' he said, and allowed the words to linger in the air a moment.

Brauns leaned forward in anticipation. 'Unless what?'

Brains rested his elbows on the arm of his chair and placed his long thin fingers together. 'Not unless we get *more* than the seven thousand pounds we're owed. Not unless we get *all* of it. All of the money from the sale of this sheep.'

Behind them, someone coughed.

Brains and Brauns swivelled round in their seats

to see Neck Brace Man loitering by the wall. He was pretending to study a framed map of Ovwick Rumble hanging by the end of the bar, but he must have been there the whole time, listening to their conversation.

'It's funny you should mention that,' Neck Brace Man whispered to them. 'For I've been thinking the very same thing.'

He grabbed a bar stool, plonked it down by Brauns, and took a seat at the table. 'Why should that little boy and his family get the lion's share of the money?'

'They're not selling a lion,' Brauns butted in. 'It's a sheep.'

Neck Brace Man ignored him. 'I've wasted time and energy travelling all the way up to Scotland, waiting for my measly three thousand pounds. Why don't we take the sheep, and set up our own auction, somewhere far, far away?'

'Portsmouth?' Brauns asked.

'Exactly,' Neck Brace Man replied. 'Or the Isle of Wight. The Mull of Kintyre, I don't care. Just somewhere no one knows us. Then we'll get *all* the money. The whole sixty thousand pounds. We can do what we like with that.'

Brauns gasped in delight. 'A B and B?'

An easy smile broke across Neck Brace Man's face. He looked more relaxed too. He had fewer lines around his eyes. The past two weeks in Ovwick Rumble had clearly done him the world of good. He was dressed in a polo shirt and white trousers, having splurged on some new holiday clothes. His blond hair looked a shade lighter, his face had caught the sun, and he'd been able to work on his tan. Not *every* day, obviously, this being Scotland. 'Sure,' he said. 'Why not? You can buy a B and B.'

Brains had kept very quiet during this whole exchange. He smoothed down his hair. Picked a piece of fluff off his jumper. 'And how do you propose we do all this?' he said eventually.

Neck Brace Man looked all about him to check that no one could hear. Then he nodded to Jimmy. 'We break into his farm first thing on the day of the auction, and steal the sheep. Then we hot-foot it down to the Isle of Wight, or wherever we're going—'

'Why does it have to be an isle?' Brauns interrupted. 'I don't like going on ferries.'

Brains held up his hand to silence Brauns. 'Carry on,' he said to Neck Brace Man.

'We break into Argonaut Farm, and steal the sheep,' Neck Brace Man repeated. 'We'll do it when they're all sleeping. It's simple, really.' There was something so casual in his manner, in what he was saying, as if it was going to be as easy as pie.

'Why not tomorrow?' Brauns asked.

'Reconnaissance, my friend,' Neck Brace Man replied. Brauns didn't have the foggiest what he meant. 'We can't just blunder in, we need to set things in place. We need to check out the layout, work out an escape plan. Go over our exit strategy. In other words, tomorrow we'll do a stakeout.'

Brauns' eyes glazed over. 'Steak?' he whispered. His stomach rumbled. It had been at least an hour since his calamari and chips.

'And how do we sell the sheep?' Brains asked coolly.

Neck Brace Man raised an eyebrow. 'I'm sure that between us, we know someone who can help us. Don't tell me you don't know someone who can shift property that you've, uh, *acquired*?'

Brains looked at him for a moment, then nodded. 'I've got someone in mind,' he replied.

Neck Brace Man sat up, looking rather pleased with himself. 'Excellent. Excellent! Well then, that's settled. I'll see you two gentlemen at the farm to-morrow, shall I? Say, eight o'clock?'

Brains nodded. 'We'll see you there.'

Brauns nodded. 'For steak,' he added.

Neck Brace Man got up from his stool and bid them good night.

Brains watched him walk the length of the bar and through the door to the stairs that led to the bedrooms. He smiled across at Brauns. 'The game is afoot,' he said, a mysterious twinkle in his eye.

Brauns smiled right back at Brains, unable to believe he was going to get steak *and* a sheep. This really was turning out to be the best holiday ever.

Neck Brace Man climbed the stairs to his room. He smiled to himself, unable to believe just how gullible the two men had been.

CHAPTER FIFTEEN

The first *CRRRAASSSSH!!!* Charlie heard from downstairs woke him immediately, and he sat bolt upright in bed. Wiping sleep from his eyes, he noticed that Jimmy's camp bed in the corner of the room remained untouched. By the fifth crash, Charlie was well and truly awake. So was the rest of the household, and everyone padded downstairs to see what all the noise was about.

That's when they saw Jimmy, hunched over one of his dad's wellies – the left one – holding his stomach with one hand.

And that's when they noticed the owl strapped to his other arm. A tawny owl with a pinched yellow beak and huge yellow eyes, taking in the room he'd suddenly found himself in.

'WHAT THE BLAZES IS GOING ON?' Charlie's dad boomed in a voice so loud the whole of Ovwick Rumble would have heard it. 'AND WHAT THE BLAZES IS THAT?'

Jimmy stood up slowly, and wiped his mouth with the back of his hand. His *free* hand, obviously, not the one with the owl attached. 'It's an owl,' he stated simply.

'I KNOW IT'S A FLAMING OWL!' his dad boomed. 'BUT I WANT TO KNOW WHAT THE BLAZES IS IT DOING IN MY HOUSE?'

Jimmy beamed proudly. 'I got given him.'

His mum's eyebrows shot up. 'What?'

Jimmy shrugged nonchalantly. 'It's no big deal,' he said. 'Someone asked if I wanted an owl, and I know Dad's always saying he wants more exotic animals on the farm. So I thought, all right, it's not a llama, but it's a start.'

His dad spluttered incredulously. 'You got given him? An owl?' This was clearly too much for him to comprehend. 'From who? Who brings an owl to the pub?'

Jimmy shrugged. 'Some guy who was there for

Debbie's birthday drinks.' He gazed into the owl's eyes. The owl blinked slowly back at him. 'We'll call him Fred. Fred the owl.'

'All the animals' names have a sporting theme,' Charlie piped up.

'Where are we gonna put him?' Uncle Martin enquired. He thought for a moment. 'He could go in the barn, I suppose. That's where everyone else is.'

Charlie's dad marched over to his wellies. He peered inside, then recoiled at what he saw. 'For goodness' sake, Jimmy,' he cried. 'You're cleaning those out first thing tomorrow morning.'

'Eddie the Eagle!' Uncle Martin blurted out from nowhere. 'You know, that rubbish ski jumper. And all right, he's not an eagle, but he's got feathers, so it's sort of the same?'

The owl let out a timely hoot then, so that settled it.

Jimmy grinned. 'Hey, Charlie,' he said, beaming. 'I was having a little chat with Eddie the Eagle here, earlier, and he said he'd only gone and got married last week. I said, "You twit. To who?"'

Charlie grinned as Jimmy roared with laughter. 'You twit, to who!' he repeated.

Uncle Martin scratched his head. 'I don't get it,' he said. 'Where's his wife, then?'

Charlie's dad let out a big huff. 'For goodness' sake,' he cried. 'Sometimes I think I'm the only one in this family who *wants* Argonaut Farm to succeed. It may have escaped your notice, but we are selling a world-famous sheep in' – he checked the clock on the mantelpiece – 'about thirty hours' time, and you stumble home like this. Honestly.'

He wrapped his dressing gown tighter around him and stomped up the stairs to bed.

Charlie's mum trailed behind him, but turned back to look at Jimmy. 'You know,' she sighed, shooting him a tight smile. 'Spending hours in the pub, returning home with unusual animals – you two are more alike than you realize.'

Uncle Martin trudged back upstairs, leaving Charlie alone with Jimmy. 'He needs to lighten up,' Jimmy huffed, nodding his head towards the stairs. 'You'd have thought I'd stolen a fleet of cars every single day I've been here the way he goes on at me.'

'He's just being Dad, you know,' Charlie replied.

Jimmy nodded, relenting. 'I know,' he agreed. 'But it doesn't half get on my wick.' He clutched at his chest, stifling a burp. 'You'd have thought he'd be grateful I won Eddie the Eagle. I'm adding to his menagerie.'

Charlie thought for a moment, looking from Jimmy to the owl. '*Won* him?' he said eventually. 'Won him how?'

Jimmy shook his head. 'I didn't mean that.'

But there was something about his shifty look that Charlie didn't trust. 'Won him?' he repeated. Something twigged in his mind. 'You won him in a bet, didn't you?'

Jimmy held up his free hand in protest. 'Not me, guv'nor,' he said with a hiccup.

'You won him in a bet,' Charlie repeated. He could feel his cheeks growing hot. 'I can't believe it. We said no gambling!' He turned to march back upstairs. 'I'm telling Dad.'

'Don't!' Jimmy cried. He let out a long sigh. 'All right, look,' he said after a moment. 'Yes, I won

Eddie the Eagle in a bet. But it was just a silly little game, that's all. It wasn't poker, or anything. There weren't any cards involved.'

'It could have been Snap for all I care!' Charlie shot back. 'That's not the point. Dad said no bets. No gambling.' He couldn't believe how angry he felt.

'It was just a stupid little bet, Charlie,' Jimmy muttered. 'It doesn't mean I'm gonna go off the rails again.'

Charlie folded his arms. He didn't want to hear his brother's excuses.

But still. Maybe Jimmy *was* trying to change. Maybe this was just a one-off.

He sighed. 'Don't do anything like that again, all right?' he said softly. 'Otherwise it'll be game over. Don't give Dad any reason to throw you out or send you to live with Cousin Graham again. I don't want that to happen. I like having you here.'

'Game. Over,' Jimmy said, suppressing another burp. 'Got it.'

He looked at Charlie for a moment, his face

suddenly serious. 'I like being here,' he replied. 'I won't let it happen. I promise.'

He beamed right at Charlie. And then he held his stomach and turned once more to empty the contents of it into Dad's wellie – the right one, this time.

'Gross!' Charlie whispered, before climbing the stairs to bed.

'Too-wit. Too-wit,' Eddie the Eagle chirped in agreement.

CHAPTER SIXTEEN

Bright and early the next morning, the Rudge family were frantically preparing for the auction the following day. Dad and Uncle Martin were at the front gate, hammering a wooden sign into the ground. It read: ARGONAUT FARM SHEEP AUCTION. SATURDAY AT 10 A.M. FAMOUS FLEECE. ONCE-IN-A-LIFETIME EVENT!

Uncle Martin took a Sharpie pen from his pinny and added *Check Your Shoes at the Gate* to the board.

'What does that mean?' Charlie's dad asked him.

'You'll see.' Uncle Martin grinned.

Jimmy and his mum were in the tea room, cleaning, baking, tidying, decorating and generally doing everything they could to spruce the place up.

Jimmy looked like death. He had bags under his eyes and a throbbing pain behind them. His stomach felt like it was doing a million somersaults a minute.

Charlie was in the barn checking on the animals before he left for school. He wanted to make sure that Eddie the Eagle was settling in OK. The owl was perched on one of the low beams running across the roof of the barn. He didn't look too perplexed, so Charlie figured he was all right.

And sitting in the front seat of a battered beige Citroën on the very edge of Argonaut Farm, watching everything through a pair of binoculars, were Brains and Brauns.

'Can I have a go?' Brauns asked, holding out his hand. He'd only had a quick look through them and that had been half an hour ago. His stomach rumbled. 'Where are the steaks?'

At that moment, the back door of the car opened, and Brains and Brauns turned to see the man in the neck brace slide into the back seat.

'Morning, chaps,' Neck Brace Man said.

'At last,' Brauns said, clapping his hands in delight. 'Now we can eat!'

Neck Brace Man looked at him curiously for a moment, and then turned to Brains. 'What have you found out?'

Brains wordlessly passed him his notebook, and Neck Brace Man took it all in. Brains had sketched a complete diagram of Argonaut Farm; there was the farmhouse, the farmyard, the field, the stables, the barn where the animals lived, and an unidentified potting shed with a dodgy door round the back.

A buzzing sound from the direction of the barn caused them all to peer across the farm. Brains squinted through the binoculars once more. Charlie, Jimmy and Charlie's dad were struggling to get hold of a sheep and sit him upright. The boy held a vibrating pair of shears in his hand. A black-and-white dog was running around them, barking in delight.

Neck Brace Man passed Brains the notebook. 'I think we're all good to go,' he said. 'We take the sheep, we exit the sheep pen, come down the dirt track, back to the car that we'll park here, we drive off, straight down the M8, and we don't look back.'

Brains nodded. 'Sounds like a plan.'

Neck Brace Man ran a hand through his hair, all casual. 'Excellent. Excellent. Well, then. Why don't we come here at, say, five o'clock? The crack of dawn. Before that lot are up, anyway.'

Brauns thought for a moment. 'No,' he said, shaking his head. 'No, no, no. Nope. No. That won't work at all.'

Neck Brace Man stared at him in surprise. 'What? It's what we agreed last night.'

'I don't go anywhere in the morning without an omelette first of all,' Brauns replied, matter-of-factly. 'Six egg. It's gotta be a six-egg omelette. Ain't that right, Brains?'

Brains rolled his eyes. 'It's true. He's useless of a morning without his breakfast.'

Neck Brace Man sighed. 'Well, we can't go too late, else we'll risk being seen. Can't you just have a slice of toast? Or a bowl of muesli?'

'A BOWL OF MUESLI?' Brauns spluttered, incredulous. 'A *bowl*? Of *muesli*? I can't bash people's heads in on a bowl of muesli! Next you'll be telling me, *Oh, have a banana! Here, have a handful of goji berries and be done with it. Look at this splendid Ryvita,*

that'll fill you up. Oh, look, three grapes and a bran flake.
Whatever next!'

Brains held up his hand to silence him. 'We'll get
to the farm at five tomorrow morning, don't worry.'

Neck Brace Man held Brains' gaze for a moment
before nodding, satisfied with the answer. 'Good.
I'll meet you here. It won't do for us to risk being
seen leaving together. People might suspect we were
up to something.'

As if on cue, right at that moment there was a
loud *knock* on the car window.

Brains, Brauns and Neck Brace Man all jumped
in their seats.

Charlie's dad leaned down and peered through
the window.

'Oh God,' Brauns whispered. 'Oh God, all right,
don't panic. Nobody panic. And nobody move! He
can't see us if we don't move!'

'It's a bit late for that,' Neck Brace Man hissed
from the back seat.

Brains wound down the window. 'Can we help
you?' he asked. He set his face to look blank, inno-
cent, and not at all like they'd just been plotting

to steal the farm's most prized possession.

'That's what I was going to ask you!' Charlie's dad grumbled. 'What are you doing here? You'll get your money tomorrow, you know you will.'

Brains nodded. 'That's as may be, Mr Rudge,' he said smoothly. 'We didn't think it would do any harm to check up on our investment.'

'Hmph,' he replied. 'Hmph.'

''Ere,' Brauns piped up. 'You wanna tell that lad of yours to get a strong grip on the sheep's head if he wants to shear him. That's what I do when I'm squeezing people's heads to a pulp and don't want them to wriggle off. A nice firm grip, that's what you need. Tell him to use the crook of his elbow, if he has to.'

Charlie's dad instinctively rubbed his own head, as if remembering exactly what it felt like to be trapped in Brauns' vice-like grip. 'Right,' he said, unconvinced. 'I'll pass that on. Er, thanks, I guess.'

Brauns beamed at him. 'No problem,' he said. 'We're having steak in a bit. Fancy joining us?'

'Are we?' Neck Brace Man piped up.

'Yeah,' Brauns said, swivelling round in his seat

to look at him. 'You said this was a stakeout. So where's the steaks?'

'Yes, thank you,' Brains said in a fake, sing-songy voice and he quickly rolled the window back up. 'Good day to you!'

Mr Rudge stepped back out of the way as Brains quickly started the engine and steered the car out of the farm.

'You're flaming nuts!' Brains yelled at Brauns as the car careered over the dirt track and away from Argonaut Farm. 'Fancy telling the person we're stealing the sheep from that we're checking out how to steal the sheep from him.'

Brauns didn't quite understand what he'd done wrong, but he had the sneaking suspicion that there was now no question of having steak, and that, quite possibly, it had never even been on the menu.

Ten minutes later, Brains pulled up outside the Golden Fleece pub and cut the engine. 'Five o'clock at the farm, tomorrow,' Neck Brace Man said. 'And keep your mouths shut!' He clambered out of the car and walked into the pub.

As soon as he was out of sight, Brains leaned in

to whisper conspiratorially. 'Now listen very carefully,' he hissed. 'And don't repeat a word of this to anyone. We're going to get up an hour earlier than we've just said we would, all right?'

Brauns didn't understand, but he had the vague notion that he was going to get less sleep than he'd previously thought. 'Why?'

'Because we're going to sneak into Argonaut Farm and get the sheep on our own. Without that man.'

'Why?'

Brains let out a sigh. He'd grown quite fond of hanging about with Brauns. They'd had a lovely time on this extended holiday of theirs, he was a super person to visit museums with, and he was ever so handy with his fists if they got into a spot of bother, but it wasn't half hard work having to explain everything all the time. 'Because then we'll get to keep *all* of the money,' he stated matter-of-factly. 'And we won't have to give that man a bean.'

Brauns mulled this over for a moment. 'Wouldn't we be giving him cash?' he asked.

Brains could stand it no longer. He undid his

seatbelt and opened the car door. 'We're not going to be giving him anything,' he hissed. 'We're stealing the sheep, just the two of us, so we'll get the whole sixty thousand pounds. We just have to make sure that we get to the farm well before the time we told him we would. All right?'

Brains climbed out of the car and started walking towards the pub.

This was all too much for Brauns to take in. In fact, only one thought popped into his head after all that. 'But what about my six-egg omelette?' he called. 'That had better not go the way of the steaks!'

But it was too late – Brains had gone.

That night, Charlie was lying in bed, trying to sleep. No matter how tightly he squeezed his eyes shut, he just couldn't. It didn't help that Uncle Martin kept playing his Michael Bublé songs over and over in his room while he was on eBay selling a jar of Michael Bublé's sweat, either. It didn't help that Charlie had seen Uncle Martin in the bathroom wiping his own sweat into a jar, having obviously got carried away with faking things to sell.

Charlie's mind just wouldn't stop whirring. His stomach kept flipping over, like it did when he rode on rollercoasters, or travelled a number of floors in a lift. His mind kept flipping over too, thinking of all the things that could go wrong at the auction the next day.

'Can't sleep?' Jimmy called to him. Charlie turned to look at him in his camp bed. Jimmy had both arms resting behind his head, staring up at the ceiling. 'Me neither.'

'What if it all goes wrong?' Charlie whispered.

'Of course it won't,' Jimmy said. 'Why would it?'

You don't know the half of it, Charlie thought. He let out a big puff of air. Was what he was doing really naughty? Uncle Martin had called him a criminal mastermind. What if everyone found out he'd lied and cheated and faked his way through it all? Would he have to go to prison if he was caught? Oh, no. Would he have to go to Cleethorpes?

'I really can't thank you enough, Charlie,' Jimmy said, interrupting his thoughts. 'For selling Alan

Shearer, for me.' He took a deep breath. 'I'm sorry it's all come to this.'

Charlie didn't say anything to that. In the darkness, he could hear the sound of Jimmy sniffing, and then blowing his nose.

'Hey, you know what will get you off to sleep, don't you?' Jimmy said after a moment.

'Hearing Mum talk about make-up?' Charlie replied. 'Hearing Dad talk about Southend United? Hearing Uncle Martin talk about Michael flaming Bublé and his jar of sweat?'

'Yes,' Jimmy said. 'All of those things. But I meant the old tried-and-tested method.' He grinned at him. 'Just try counting sheep. Lord knows we've got enough of 'em.'

That's the problem, Charlie thought. *And I've worked it so that you don't know which one is which.* He squeezed his eyes shut and tried to block out the images flashing through his mind of Alan Shearer, Alan Shearer Two (Jessica Ennis-Hill) and a SWAT team arresting Charlie and carting him off in a hearse to Cleethorpes.

CHAPTER SEVENTEEN

The birds were singing, the sun was beginning to rise and wispy clouds scudded across the sky as Neck Brace Man strode up the dirt track to Argonaut Farm just after four o'clock on Saturday morning. He clambered over the front garden gate and tiptoed across to the barn.

He laughed as he thought how slack the security on the farm was, for the door to the barn was merely closed, not locked. He slid the door open, and stepped inside.

'Oh!' he exclaimed, startled at what he saw.

For there, in the middle of the sheep pen, with a bleating sheep in his arms, was Brauns. On the other side of the pen, pointing at the various sheep, was Brains.

They turned in surprise when they heard Neck Brace Man, and looked like a pair of rabbits caught in headlights.

'Wh-what are you doing here?' Neck Brace Man spluttered.

Brains narrowed his eyes at him. 'I could ask you the same question. We agreed we'd meet here at five o'clock.'

Neck Brace Man looked at his watch. It was quarter past four. 'Then why are *you* here?'

'I asked first,' Brains replied.

'No you didn't.'

'Uh—' Brauns stuttered, for the rest of the sheep were beginning to nibble at his shoes. He passed Alan Shearer Two (Jessica Ennis-Hill) over the top of the sheep pen to Brains, who placed her down on the ground. From his pocket, Brains took a length of rope with one end fashioned into a lasso.

'Coming here early, taking the sheep without me so you haven't got to give me my share,' Neck Brace Man grumbled. 'You're trying to fleece me!'

Brains placed the looped rope around Alan Shearer Two (Jessica Ennis-Hill)'s neck. 'No, no, no,' he insisted, holding up his hands in protest. 'You've got it all wrong. We were going to get the sheep, bring it back to the pub, knock for you, and then all three of us would have been on our merry way.'

'Uh—' Brauns stuttered again, but Brains and Neck Brace Man ignored him.

'Like *that's* the truth,' Neck Brace Man hissed. He stepped nearer to them and clenched his fists. 'You were trying to do me over.'

Brains looked at the man's hands. 'Oh, like that, is it? Very well, if it's a fight you're after.' He nodded to Brauns.

'Uh—' Brauns repeated.

Brains laughed at him. 'What's the matter, Brauns?' he said. 'You're not wimping out from fighting *him,* are you? After all you've done?'

Brauns shook his head. 'No, it's just—'

'Well, then,' Brains laughed. 'That's settled. Out you come.' He held out his hand and helped Brauns clamber over the sheep-pen gate.

Neck Brace Man squared up to him and straightened his tie. 'Before we start,' he said, 'maybe we ought to lay down a few ground rules. Make this fair, you know?'

Brains narrowed his eyes. 'Go on.'

Neck Brace Man slicked down his hair. 'Right. Well. Um. No biting. No hair pulling. No boxing the ears. No spitting. No, um, diving. No bombing. No heavy petting. No wedgies. No Chinese burns. And no name-calling. It's just not very nice.'

'Uh—' Brauns stuttered for the hundredth time.

Brains nodded. 'We do this for the sheep. Who-ever wins the fight gets to keep the sheep and all the money. Deal?'

Neck Brace Man reached round the back of his neck and detached the neck brace. He placed it on the floor of the barn.

Brains looked at him in astonishment, but Neck Brace Man – well, he wasn't actually in the neck brace at the moment – the man formerly known as Neck Brace Man shrugged. 'I'm not actually injured,' he whispered conspiratorially. 'I just wear that thing to make it look like I am. To make it seem like Jimmy did me a real injury and therefore owes me money.'

'You're trying to fleece Jimmy!' Brains cried, astonished, but it wasn't as if he could take the moral high ground.

The man formerly known as Neck Brace Man held up his clenched fists. 'Put 'em up,' he purred. 'Put 'em up.'

Brauns sighed. 'I'd love to,' he said wearily. 'Honestly. I'd love nothing more than a good old fight. You know me. There's just one problem.'

Brains looked at him incredulously. 'What?' he boomed. 'What on earth could *possibly* be the matter?'

'The sheep's gone,' Brauns stated matter-of-factly.

'What?'

Brauns nodded to the sheep pen. 'It ran off. About five minutes ago. I did try and tell you.'

Brains and the man formerly known as Neck Brace Man turned to look at where Brains had placed Alan Shearer Two (Jessica Ennis-Hill). And, true enough, she was no longer there.

The sheep had escaped!

'Oh, for goodness' sake!' Brains cried. 'After that blasted sheep!'

All three of them raced towards the door. Brains and the man formerly known as Neck Brace Man got there at the exact same time, and barged and chivvied each other out of the way to be the first one through it.

Brauns powered through behind them, pushing all three of them out of the door. They shot out into the farmyard, just in time to see Alan Shearer Two (Jessica Ennis-Hill), the lassoed rope trailing in her wake, making a run for it over by the empty stables.

'Onwards!' Brains cried, and all three of them pegged it after the sheep.

The man formerly known as Neck Brace Man stuck out his foot and Brains tripped over it. He went flying across the farmyard. The man formerly known as Neck Brace Man leaped over Brains, lying in a heap on the floor, and ploughed on after the sheep.

He chased Alan Shearer Two (Jessica Ennis-Hill) all the way to a ditch at the edge of the farm.

He came to a stop as he saw the sheep tottering on the very brink of the ditch. 'There, there,' the man formerly known as Neck Brace Man soothed. 'That's it. Nice and easy. Good sheep. This way. Good sheep.' He inched his way forward, arms outstretched, ready to snatch the sheep.

But just at that moment, Brains and Brauns came barrelling over. The man formerly known as Neck Brace Man raised his hands in protest. 'Stop!' he shrieked. 'Stop!'

But it was too late. Brauns couldn't slow down in time, and he accidentally barged right into the man formerly known as Neck Brace Man. He teetered on the spot for a moment, before tipping forward and knocking into Alan Shearer Two (Jessica Ennis-Hill), who in turn teetered on the edge of the ditch for a moment, before pitching forward and tumbling down into it.

'Noooooooooo!' Brains, Brauns and the man formerly known as Neck Brace Man all cried in unison.

'BAAAAAAAAAAAAAAAAAaaaaaaaaaaaaaaa!!!!!!' Alan Shearer Two (Jessica Ennis-Hill) bleated in despair, her cry growing fainter the further she fell.

CRAAAAAASSSSSSSH!

All three men stepped forward and peered over the top of the ditch. To their relief, the sheep was fine, for it had landed on a soft mound of earth, almost like a ledge, halfway down the ditch. It bleated away in bemusement.

'Pheeewwww!' Brauns whistled. 'I don't want to be no sheep murderer.'

Brains wiped his forehead. 'That's all very well,' he reasoned. 'But someone needs to go down there and fetch it back.'

All three peered into the ditch again. It seemed an awfully long way down. Ever since they'd moved to Argonaut Farm, Charlie's mum had moaned to Charlie's dad that the ditch was a potential death trap and needed to be filled in for *precisely* this reason. Though to be fair, Charlie's dad could never have predicted three men would be trying to steal a faked sheep.

'I'm not going down there,' the man formerly known as Neck Brace Man grumbled.

'Nor me,' said Brauns.

'Nor me,' said Brains.

The three of them stood looking at one another

for several moments, no one quite sure what to do.

Eventually, Brains huffed. 'Well, someone has to,' he said. 'That's our goldmine down there.'

A sudden thought struck the man formerly known as Neck Brace Man. 'Rock, Paper, Scissors?' he asked, holding out a clenched fist.

Brains rolled his eyes in despair. Had his years of underhand deeds, petty criminal activity and mental training in the form of daily crosswords and sudokus *really* come to this?

The man formerly known as Neck Brace Man held out a clenched fist. 'On three. One.'

'Two,' Brains chanted.

'Six,' Brauns chipped in. Counting wasn't his strong point.

'Three!' the man formerly known as Neck Brace Man corrected.

And with that, Brains gave him an almighty shove and he plummeted down into the ditch.

'AAAAAAAAARRRRGGGGGGGHHHH!' he cried as he fell to the bottom and landed awkwardly with a heavy thud.

And then—

SNAAAAAAAAPP!

'THAT WAS MY ARM! YOU'VE BROKEN MY ARM!'

Brains and Brauns peered over the top of the ditch to see the man formerly known as Neck Brace Man slumped in a heap at the bottom. His face was contorted in pain as he cradled his left arm in his right.

Brains rolled his eyes. 'You've probably just sprained it,' he called down.

'I've got brittle bones!' the man formerly known as Neck Brace Man yelled back. He shifted his weight to try to stand up.

SNAAAAAAAAPP!

'YEEEEE-OOOWWWW!' the man formerly known as Neck Brace Man yelled. 'THAT WAS MY LEG! I'VE BROKEN MY LEG! WHAT FRESH HELL IS THIS?'

He collapsed in a heap once more. 'Please!' he whimpered, his voice as broken as two of his limbs. 'Please help me.'

Brauns thought for a moment. 'Hang on!' he yelled down. 'Just wait there!'

'Oh, really?' the man formerly known as Neck Brace Man called back. 'I'd had it in mind to go skydiving. Maybe followed by a nice safari trip chasing wild elephants. Then, if I've time, I wouldn't mind running a marathon.'

Brauns looked at him in surprise. 'Really?'

'NO!' the man formerly known as Neck Brace Man yelled. 'Of course not! Where the flaming heck do you think I'm gonna go? "Wait there," he says. Honestly. Of all the things—'

Brauns frowned. 'There's no need to be so rude. I'm trying to help.' And with that, he ran off back in the direction of the barn.

Brains was left standing at the top of the ditch all on his own. He looked down at the man formerly known as Neck Brace Man. The man formerly known as Neck Brace Man stared right back at him. Neither said anything for a while.

Brains let out a low whistle. He couldn't think of a single thing to say. He stroked his moustache, the minutes taking an eternity to pass. Then, something came to him:

'Going anywhere nice for your holidays this

year?' he said, trying to pass the time with small talk and chit-chat.

The man formerly known as Neck Brace Man shrugged. 'I was thinking Corfu,' he replied. 'But we'll have to see how it goes.'

'Oh, right,' Brains replied brightly. 'Yes, I've heard it's nice there. Great food. Beautiful buildings.'

The conversation dried up once more. Brains looked up to the heavens, wishing Brauns would hurry up. This was all getting rather awkward.

After a few more moments of silence, Brauns came racing back, stopping right at the edge of the ditch to catch his breath. 'Here!' he cried and he held aloft the man formerly known as Neck Brace Man's neck brace. 'Have this!'

Brauns flung the neck brace into the ditch and it fluttered down to where the man was lying. 'What good's this going to do me?' the man cried. 'I've broken my arm and my leg. Not my neck.'

Brauns frowned. 'Well, there's gratitude for you.'

The man formerly known as Neck Brace Man sighed, but picked up the neck brace nonetheless. With his one good arm, he put it back round his neck. 'Better than nothing, I suppose,' the man (now back) in the neck brace grumbled.

At that moment, a sharp cry rang out from the farmhouse.

Brains and Brauns looked over, and made out Uncle Martin, rake in hand, prowling round the barn. He'd discovered that Alan Shearer Two (Jessica Ennis-Hill) was missing. Now they were for it!

'We've gotta go!' Brains cried, grabbing Brauns by the arm and preparing to run.

'Wait!' Neck Brace Man cried. 'You can't leave me!'

'We're sorry!' Brains hissed. 'But they're awake. It's the boy's uncle. He'll discover us any minute.'

'What about me?' Neck Brace Man yelled.

But Brains and Brauns had already gone, dashing down the dirt track and back to the safety of the Golden Fleece.

CHAPTER EIGHTEEN

Uncle Martin's cry had alerted Charlie, and he raced to the barn to see what all the shouting was about. There he found Uncle Martin leaning over the gate of the sheep pen, his head in his hands. 'Uncle Martin?' he asked. 'What's the matter?'

Uncle Martin shook his head. 'It's Alan Shearer. She's gone.'

Charlie gasped. 'No!' he cried. 'No, she can't have. She was in the potting shed.' His stomach already felt like it was lined with lead wrapped up in concrete, and now this.

Uncle Martin thought for a moment. 'Oh, no, sorry,' he replied. 'I meant Alan Shearer Two. Jessica Ennis-Hill. *She's* gone.'

Charlie let out a sigh of relief. Granted, he wasn't

particularly pleased that Jessica Ennis-Hill had gone a-wandering, but at least it wasn't Alan Shearer, his pride and joy.

Then another thought struck him.

'But today's the auction!' he cried, clasping his hand over his mouth as the realization set in. 'What are we going to do?'

Uncle Martin shrugged. 'We could auction Alan Shearer? The real one. Seeing as whoever bids for her won't get to take her away till after the competition tomorrow. We could try and find Jessica Ennis-Hill by then?'

'No,' Charlie stated firmly. 'It's too risky. People might notice the difference.' He looked at his uncle. 'Not that I'm saying your graffiti isn't excellent. We just can't take the chance.'

Uncle Martin nodded. 'Fair enough.' He looked around the pen and counted the rest of the sheep – Muhammad Ali, Maria Sharapova and a half-shorn David Beckham. 'Same as before, then?' he offered.

It took Charlie a moment to work out what he meant. And then it dawned on him. 'You mean, fake *another* sheep? Alan Shearer Three?'

Uncle Martin nodded. 'There's nothing else for it. You want to auction a sheep, don't you? To get money for Jimmy? So Mick can expand the farm? So I can have my two tea rooms?'

Charlie nodded. He needed to make sure the auction went ahead for *all* those reasons. And, most importantly, so that he could keep the real Alan Shearer and use her in his bid to be crowned Young Farmer of the Year at the competition the next day.

'So that's settled, then.' Uncle Martin gave Charlie a tight smile. 'I'll get the spray-paint.'

He turned back to the sheep pen. 'Let's see. This time, we'll go for . . .' He looked at the various sheep, trying to choose. Charlie could have sworn they all shrank back a bit from his gaze, as if they knew what Uncle Martin was planning.

'Maria Sharapova,' Uncle Martin said firmly after a moment. 'It's your lucky day.'

Maria Sharapova let out a small bleat, almost like a whimper. Funnily enough, she didn't feel lucky at all.

CHAPTER NINETEEN

Argonaut Farm had never seen so many people traipsing through the gates. It seemed to Charlie like the flock of spectators flooding in would never stop. And they were all so excited to be there! To witness a real life *Homes Under the Hammer*. But with sheep. And no hammers.

Uncle Martin was having a terribly difficult time at the front gate, making everyone dip their shoes into disinfectant, for he'd researched on the internet that that was required when such a large number of people were trampling all over your field. Everyone grumbled that the line was moving too slowly, and that Uncle Martin should just hurry up, else they'd be there all day. One woman moaned because she was wearing flip-flops and Uncle Martin made her dunk her bare feet into the bowl, her toes going blue from the liquid.

But what was even more incredible than the sheer number of people rocking up at Argonaut Farm was that many were taking the opportunity of the auction to offload any old things they had lying round. Mrs Morrison from the farm next door had brought a set of gardening tools she wanted to get rid of. An elderly man had brought a set of steak knives he'd won on a game show. Seven people brought a chicken they wanted to sell. One chap lugged in a fridge freezer.

Charlie let out a puff of air. It was all very well these people turning up – who knows, it might even help with the bidding for Alan Shearer; the price for her could keep going up and up. The only sticking point was, the longer the auction took, the more chance there was for something to go wrong. What if someone noticed that Alan Shearer Three (Maria Sharapova) wasn't Alan Shearer? What if it rained and Alan Shearer Three (Maria Sharapova)'s black spray-paint came off? What if Alan Shearer Three (Maria Sharapova) suddenly learned to talk and revealed that she was, in fact, an imposter? Charlie knew that this was unlikely, granted, but he was so nervous, his mind couldn't stop whirring with such fantastical thoughts and incredible scenarios. Still, he reasoned, if Alan Shearer Three (Maria Sharapova) *did* suddenly learn to talk, they'd have bigger things to think about than her spilling the beans. They'd have a talking sheep, for starters. They could go on the road and tour as the World's First Sheep-and-Boy performers. They could go on *Britain's Got Talent*! Besides, Alan Shearer Three (Maria Sharapova) didn't seem like a snitch. David Beckham on the other hand. Hmm. He'd always thought David Beckham looked a bit suspect.

'Shut. Up,' Charlie hissed to himself, and he tapped the side of his head to try and get these ridiculous thoughts to stop whirring around it.

'What, love?' his mum said. She, Charlie's dad and Jimmy were standing next to him, also amazed at the number of people at their farm. And there, at the front of the crowd, was Saul Hoskins, standing with his mum and dad and a group of other farmers. Saul gave Charlie a little smirk, and mouthed 'This sheep's gonna be mine,' at him.

Charlie narrowed his eyes and turned back to his family. 'Nothing,' he said to his mum. 'I just want to get on with it.'

'Coo-eee!' a voice trilled behind them. They turned to see Debbie from Debbie & Dale's Dairy & Baked Goods Emporium tottering her way towards them in a mini skirt, low-cut top and bright pink high heels. She pursed her lips into her best pout when she saw Jimmy.

Jimmy, for his part, gulped nervously and turned as red as sunburn.

'Mutton dressed as lamb,' Charlie's mum muttered under her breath, but everyone heard her.

Eloise paced a couple of steps behind her mum, clearly embarrassed. She looked over at Jimmy shyly, and Jimmy smiled back. Charlie rolled his eyes. Had they even actually had a conversation yet?

At that moment, Mr Partridge, the official who had verified Alan Shearer just a few weeks ago, walked over to them. He shook Charlie's dad's hand heartily. 'Lovely day for it,' he mused. 'And just look at the turnout!'

Charlie's parents and Jimmy all nodded in agreement. 'Business is booming,' Charlie's dad replied, a huge beam on his face. 'I've had to hire four lads and lasses to work in the tea room to cater for everyone.'

Mr Partridge nodded. 'That's what happens when you have an extremely rare and valuable sheep in your midst, Mr Rudge.' He looked down at his clipboard, then up at the long queue of people still snaking their way into the farm, carrying all sorts of household goods and bric-a-brac with them. 'We'd best get cracking if we're going to get through all these lots.'

A good thirty minutes later, after Uncle Martin had checked everybody in – 'WHO ON EARTH WEARS CROCS OR CLOGS OR JELLY SHOES OR SKI BOOTS TO A FARM?' he had cried – seven hundred and fifty-three people crowded onto the main field where the auction would take place.

Lurking at the back, and keeping a low profile, were Brains and Brauns. Brauns kept looking around nervously, expecting to be found out at any minute.

'Will you just calm down?' Brains hissed at

him. 'You're going to make people suspicious.'

Brauns held up his left hand to Brains. 'Just look at that,' he said. His once perfectly manicured nails had been bitten to the quick. 'This is what I've resorted to.'

Brains rolled his eyes. 'No one knows we were here,' he said. 'So stop acting so shifty.' A thought occurred to him. 'Actually, how good at acting are you?'

Brauns mulled this over for a moment. 'I was in a school play, once,' he replied. '*Romeo and Juliet.* I was the lead.'

'And?' Brains prompted.

'One reviewer said they'd never seen such a graceful and el-o-quent performer.' Brauns puffed out his chest, pleased that he'd remembered such a difficult but glowing word.

'Well, that's great,' Brains stated, pleasantly surprised. 'Well done, Romeo.'

Brauns frowned. 'I was Juliet,' he corrected.

Brains checked all around him to make sure no one could hear. 'Look,' he said. 'We have to act like we're shocked. When they announce that they're not selling the sheep.'

'Why aren't they selling the sheep?' Brauns asked. 'That's why everyone's here.'

Brains rubbed his temples. He didn't know how much longer he could live this life – ekeing out a living by dishonest means. Once this was all over, maybe he would think about opening a B&B with Brauns, after all. Anything had to be better than standing in a field, crushed by hundreds of spectators jostling around you, repeating yourself again and again to your oldest and stupidest friend. 'Yes, I know that. But there's the small matter of the sheep they're meant to be selling currently being stuck at the bottom of the ditch, along with a man with two broken limbs. Remember?'

The realization dawned on Brauns, and he nodded slowly. 'Oh, yeah,' he said. 'So they can't sell it, 'cos it's gone.'

'Right,' Brains agreed. 'But we've got to pretend we don't know anything about it. As it stands, they'll have to come up with another way of paying us the seven grand. But if they think we had anything to do with the disappearance of the sheep, we won't have a leg to stand on.'

'Just like the man in the neck brace,' Brauns mused. 'He's only got one leg to stand on, now.'

Brains looked at Brauns curiously. 'Sometimes, Brauns,' he said, 'you don't know how funny you are.'

Just then, a flurry of activity at the front of the field got their attention.

Charlie's dad was standing alongside Mr Partridge and a whole heap of bric-a-brac. Every item – or 'lot', as it was called – had a sticker with a number slapped on it. Even the chickens.

'Thank you, thank you, everyone,' Charlie's dad boomed, raising his arms to get the crowd to quieten down. Bessie weaved in between his legs, her tail thumping excitedly at all this activity.

'Yes, all right, Bess, thank you,' he said. 'Quiet now, please.' He nodded to Charlie, Charlie's mum, Jimmy and Uncle Martin. 'We all appreciate such a fantastic number of you coming to our auction today. Our really rather special auction. For today we are, as you know, selling off, for a LOT of money—'

'Uh,' Charlie interrupted. Like Cousin Graham

and his WE DO FUNERALS! GRAHAM MARKBONE: DEAD EXCITED TO HELP! sign, he didn't think that set the right sort of tone at all.

'Sorry,' Charlie's dad corrected hastily. 'We have the *privilege* of passing this rare Blackface sheep with a totally unique fleece to a new and worthy owner.'

'And don't forget the condition of sale!' Charlie piped up. 'Whoever buys Alan Shearer can't have her until after the competition tomorrow.'

Mr Partridge took over the reins. 'Very good,' he said. 'But before we get to that, our star draw, we have a number of other items to auction. So, step forward the owner of lot number one, please.'

He gestured to an old, yellowing microwave oven, which was missing the door and the timer and the button that goes *ping*. 'We'll start the bidding at one pence,' Mr Partridge sighed. Bessie barked over and over, yapping at his heels skittishly. He wiped his forehead wearily. It was going to be a long day.

CHAPTER TWENTY

*I*t turned out that approximately four hundred and seventy-three people wanted to sell their old ornaments and household goods, so it took three hours and

a trampled-on bicycle

four cracked mirrors

a broken pogo stick

seven chickens

an old cardigan

an old fleece (lined with your run-of-the-mill sheep's wool)

a well-worn nightie (flameproof)

a set of steak knives

a thermal vest

a wardrobe

a balaclava

a pair of baggy Y-fronts with loose elastic

a rolled-up tufted Wilton carpet

a year's back catalogue of *Women's Weekly*
  magazine

a hostess trolley

a food processor with several pieces of avocado
  still smeared around the edges

a holiday home in Bognor Regis

a caravan with no wheels

a dartboard with no numbers on it

a fridge freezer

an anniversary edition of Trivial Pursuit

a 1000-piece *Lord of the Rings* jigsaw puzzle with
  all the pieces making up Gandalf's face missing

and a cuddly toy

before the Rudge family FINALLY got round to selling their sheep. Which had been faked. For the second time.

Charlie's palms were sweating and his whole body was tingling with excitement, anticipation and a huge dollop of nervousness as Uncle Martin led Alan Shearer Three (Maria Sharapova) from the barn to the field.

The whole crowd gasped when they saw her. At least half of them started clicking away on their cameras and smart phones and iPads, taking as many pictures as they could of this rare and wonderful specimen. At least they weren't being charged a £1 entry fee this time. 'Cor, look at it!' someone cried.

'Isn't he beautiful?' an old woman piped up. 'What I wouldn't give to have a sheep like that!'

'She's a she,' Charlie corrected, stroking Alan Shearer Three (Maria Sharapova)'s back. Uncle Martin had done a terrific job with the spray-paint – again – copying the exact same markings as Alan Shearer onto Alan Shearer Three (Maria Sharapova)'s fleece. Charlie made a mental note to tell Uncle Martin that if the tea room didn't work out, he could totally be the new Banksy.

From the corner of his eye, Charlie could see Saul and Mr and Mrs Hoskins lurking at the front of the crowd. Mr Hoskins was whispering conspiratorially to a handful of other farmers, while Saul was still looking daggers at Charlie. Charlie took a deep breath and did his best to ignore them all.

The ripple of excitement as the sheep was led through the farm made its way to the back of the field. From where they were standing, Brains and Brauns couldn't actually see a thing. 'What's going on?' Brauns whispered. 'Why's everyone so excited?'

'It's the sheep,' the woman next to him piped up. 'They've finally brought out the Blackface ewe. And she's a beauty.'

Brains' eyebrows shot up and his mouth formed a perfect 'o'. Brauns looked at him, impressed. 'There you go!' he cried, slapping Brains on the back. 'You're a really good actor, too! You've got a terrific "surprised" face!' He thought for a moment. 'Maybe we could think about staging *Romeo and Juliet* again. I already know half the lines.'

Brains rolled his eyes. 'I've got a terrific surprised face because, funnily enough, I'm surprised,' he hissed. 'They've got the sheep.'

'And?' Brauns clearly didn't get it.

'And, if your teeny, tiny mind can possibly bear

to stretch back to this morning, or even to three hours ago when we last discussed it, we saw the sheep falling into a ditch. Remember?'

'Oh, yeah,' Brauns agreed. 'So how come it's there, then?'

Brains shrugged. 'Maybe that chap in the neck brace got him out, after all.' He searched the crowd. 'Though I can't see him anywhere.'

He stood on tiptoe, resting his hands on the shoulders of the person in front of him to hoist him up another few inches. Finally, he could see the front of the field. And there, next to the little boy and his family, stood the Blackface ewe.

Brains' mind whirred. 'That can't be it,' he whispered, almost to himself. A sudden thought occurred to him. He grinned slowly. 'Why, the sly so-and-sos,' he muttered, and he found himself impressed by their chutzpah. 'They've only gone and faked it.'

'Faked what?' Brauns asked.

'The sheep,' Brains hissed. 'Look at the evidence. This farm has only ever had one Blackface ewe worth tons of money, right? And we know that

that Blackface ewe is still lounging at the bottom of the ditch. Which means that that sheep there is *not* the Blackface ewe. They've just made it look like it is. They're going to try and fleece the bidders!'

Brauns drew himself up to his full height. 'Well, that's not right,' he said. 'We have to tell someone.'

Brains placed a hand on his arm. 'Steady on, you fool. We're not going to say a word. If we don't say anything, and that sheep gets sold, we'll get our money here and now. We won't have to wait for them to try and come up with it some other way. Get it?'

Brauns nodded slowly. 'I think so,' he said.

'And we won't get into trouble for trying to steal the thing, either. So, Mum's the word, all right?' Brains added. 'Our lips are sealed.' He drew a finger across his lips.

Brauns nodded, and did the same. 'My lips are sealed,' he repeated.

Brains smiled at him. He wasn't so bad, really, he thought. Not when you explained everything to him. Their B&B might well work after all.

At the front of the field, Mr Partridge clapped his hands in delight. 'Right, then, ladies and gentlemen. Let's get this show on the road. Who'll start the bidding at . . .' He looked from Charlie's family to the crowd. The crowd all leaned forward in anticipation.

'. . . one thousand pounds?'

A hush descended. Nobody said anything for a moment. The group of farmers standing with Mr Hoskins and Saul at the front of the crowd shuffled from one foot to the other. Two farmers were glaring at each other, psyching each other out.

'Anyone?' Mr Partridge asked, clearly surprised.

Charlie gulped. This wasn't what he had expected at all. 'Why isn't anyone bidding?' he whispered to Jimmy.

'They will, don't worry,' Jimmy soothed. 'No one wants to be seen to be that eager, that's all. It's like poker.' He placed a reassuring hand on Charlie's shoulder, but even through his jacket, Charlie could feel his hand tremble. Technically, it was Jimmy's jacket. Charlie had taken it off the coat hook by mistake that morning because he'd been so nervous about this whole day going smoothly. It was several sizes too big for him, but he had too much on his mind to be worried about that. Charlie could tell from Jimmy's trembling hand that he was resting *everything* on this auction; selling the sheep to pay off his debts and get him out of a whole heap of trouble.

'One thousand pounds!' Mr Partridge repeated. 'Come on! I hardly need to remind you all that this is one of the most rare and valuable—'

'ONE THOUSAND POUNDS!' shouted old Mrs Morrison from the farm next door. She had absolutely no intention of buying the sheep, but she couldn't bear this tension any longer.

And then, as if the floodgates had opened, that was it – they were off!

'Two thousand pounds!' one farmer cried.

'Three thousand!' yelled another.

Mr Partridge held up his hands. 'This is all very well,' he protested, 'but I must insist that *I* set the monetary values.' He smoothed down his jacket. 'Right. Thank you. Now, who'll give me four thousand pounds, do I hear four thousand?'

A hand shot up in the crowd.

'Five thousand, six, seven, there's eight, that's nine, thank you, who'll give me ten thousand?' Mr Partridge said almost in one breath as a succession of hands shot up.

Jimmy squeezed Charlie's shoulder again. 'See?' he whispered. 'I told you there was nothing to worry about.'

Charlie smiled up at him. And then he caught Uncle Martin's eye and the knot in his stomach suddenly re-appeared from nowhere. Uncle Martin shot him a tight smile, as if he knew what Charlie was thinking. Charlie squeezed his eyes shut as if trying to squeeze that sinking feeling in his stomach shut. *I'm doing it for Jimmy*, he thought silently to himself. *I'm doing it for Jimmy*. Besides, it was far too late to back out now.

'... thirty thousand,' Mr Partridge was saying, 'thirty-two, now thirty-four, thirty-six, thank you, thirty-eight ...'

At the back of the crowd, Brains squeezed Brauns' arm in delight. 'It's working!' he whispered, not quite able to believe it. 'It's actually working!'

'. . . forty-eight, who'll give me fifty thousand?' Mr Partridge cried.

Charlie's mum was nearly jumping up and down for joy. 'Fifty thousand!' she exclaimed breathlessly to Charlie's dad, unable to take it all in. You could practically see her packing for Marbella.

'Fifty thousand, thank you,' Mr Partridge repeated.

'Oh, no!' Charlie's mum cried, panicked. 'I didn't mean to bid!'

Charlie's dad laughed. 'I wouldn't worry, love,' he replied. 'I think it's doing all right without us!'

'. . . fifty-four,' Mr Partridge was saying, 'now fifty-six.'

Mr Hoskins raised his hand. 'Fifty-eight thousand,' he called.

'Fifty-eight thousand,' Mr Partridge repeated. 'Who'll give me sixty? Yep, sixty thousand pounds, thank you.'

Charlie was jostled forward by his dad and Jimmy, both patting him on the back. 'Well done, my lad!' Mr Rudge beamed. 'You've done it! You've only gone and well and truly done it!'

Even Bessie got in on the action. She started chasing her tail in circles, yapping excitedly. Charlie allowed himself to smile. Against all odds, despite all the lies, this was working.

Bessie yelped again. 'I know, Bess!' Charlie's mum called to her. 'It *is* exciting, isn't it?'

'. . . sixty-six thousand,' Mr Partridge ploughed on, 'sixty-eight, there's seventy thousand, thank you, who'll give me seventy-two, yep, seventy-two, now seventy-four. Seventy-six, now, thank you, where's seventy-eight?'

Mr Hoskins nodded.

'Seventy-eight thousand, thank you,' Mr Partridge said, 'Do I hear eighty thousand . . . ?' A farmer in the crowd held up his hat. 'Eighty thousand,' Mr Partridge confirmed. 'Thank you.'

Charlie gazed at the crowd. People were taking pictures, texting friends. A journalist was frantically filing copy for that evening's edition of *Ovwick Rumble Ramblings*. Everyone was jostling each other, trying to see everything that was going on. Toes were trodden on. Ribs had elbows dug into them. Someone accidentally stepped on Bessie's tail. She let out a small yelp, then shot off the field, darted across the farmyard and sought refuge near the disused potting shed.

'Bidding stands at eighty thousand pounds,' Mr Partridge repeated, looking from farmer to farmer. 'Any more for any more?'

Mr Hoskins made to raise his hand again, but his wife tugged at his arm. 'That's the last of the savings,' she hissed. 'We can't stretch any further.'

Saul looked up to his mum, pleading. Mr Hoskins frowned, clearly disappointed. 'We could re-mortgage,' he replied. 'I could sell a kidney.' A thought occurred to him and he looked down at Saul. 'I could sell one of the kids.'

His wife shot him such a look that he physically shrank away from her. 'Fine,' he huffed. 'Fine.'

Charlie couldn't help but grin at that. Then he held his breath in anticipation as Mr Partridge held his clipboard in the air. 'So, there we have it,' he called. 'Bidding stands at eighty thousand pounds. Going once . . .'

Jimmy gripped Charlie's shoulder tightly.

'Going twice . . .'

The crowd all looked at each other. This was it!

'SOLD!' Mr Partridge cried. 'To the man in the deerstalker hat!'

The man in the deerstalker hat stepped forward and shook his hand.

Charlie and Jimmy hugged in delight. Mr Rudge planted a smacker on his wife's lips. Uncle Martin punched his fist in the air. 'AND I'M FEEEEEEEEELING GOOOODD!' he sang at the top of his lungs, because it was his second favourite Michael Bublé song and seemed particularly fitting for the occasion.

Saul took his dad's hat, threw it on the ground and stomped all over it. 'Dad!' he whined. 'You *promised*! You promised me that sheep would be mine.' His mum tried to soothe him, but Saul couldn't stop screaming at his dad.

The crowd surged forward and patted all the Rudges on the back and shook their hands and clapped in appreciation. Charlie's head swam with the excitement of it all. They'd done it! They'd truly done it! He'd be able to keep Alan Shearer for real after all!

On a whim, Charlie reached into the pocket of his jeans and took out the tin whistle he used for Bessie's sheepdog practice. He blew into it triumphantly, and started marching around the field. Jimmy did a funny little jig next to him, and Charlie's mum and dad burst out laughing at the sheer madness of it all.

'BRILLIANT!' a man in the crowd cried.

'BEST AUCTION IN YEARS!' yelled another.

In the distance, even Bessie barked in delight. Over and over again. In fact, she wouldn't STOP barking.

'I know, Bess,' Charlie called to her over his shoulder. 'You're probably nervous at all these people. But just calm down!' He blew into his tin whistle again, three short, sharp toots.

'THIS IS BETTER THAN THE *ANTIQUES ROADSHOW*!' old Mrs Morrison shouted.

And then, amidst all the celebration and cheering and general mayhem, a voice rang out:

'WHAT'S THAT?'

Charlie stopped jigging around.

'Here!' an elderly spectator called. 'What's going on?'

Charlie took the tin whistle from his lips.

A low murmur passed through the crowd. 'Is this some sort of scam?' someone muttered. 'I can't believe it!'

Charlie gazed at them all in confusion. 'What are you talking about?'

Bessie barked again, loudly. Repeatedly. Closer, this time.

The man in the deerstalker hat marched over to Charlie's dad, pure anger etched on his face. 'What is all this?' he demanded.

Mr Rudge held up his hands in protest. 'I don't know what you mean.'

Bessie kept barking. 'Shush, girl,' he called. 'Stop with all the racket—'

And that's when they saw her.

The Rudges were the last to spot what was going on, but Charlie very quickly got the measure of it.

For rounding the corner, wagging her tail in sheer and utter delight that for once in her sorry career as a sheepdog she'd actually paid attention to

Charlie's whistles and, after weeks of practising and getting the hang of his commands, had gone ahead and managed to round up a sheep, was Bessie . . .

Shepherding a sheep onto the field.

And not just any sheep.

Not just any sheep at all.

'Alan Shearer!' Uncle Martin cried. He quickly realized his mistake. 'Uh, I mean, oh, look, I think that one's David Beckham. Or Muhammad Ali. Yes. That's it. Muhammad Ali. Good Muhammad Ali. Good sheep.'

Charlie gulped. 'Uh,' he stuttered, desperately trying to think of something to say.

The man in the deerstalker hat looked from Charlie to Alan Shearer to Alan Shearer Three (Maria Sharapova) to Mr Partridge. 'What the dickens is going on?'

'Uh,' Charlie stuttered again. He could feel beads of sweat trickling down his forehead. He stepped forward, desperately thinking of something that would sound like a plausible explanation, when a cry came from round the corner. Several cries.

'Ow!' Pause. 'Ow!' Pause. 'Ow!' Pause. 'Ow!'
Pause.

Then:

'My leg!' Pause. 'My leg!' Pause. 'My arm!'
Pause. 'My neck!'

Then:

'WHAT FRESH HELL IS THIS? WHAT
FRESH HELL IS THIS? WHAT. FRESH. HELL.
IS. THIS?'

And all of a sudden, hobbling round the corner
with one good leg and a sheep tucked under his
arm – his non-broken arm – was Neck Brace Man.

The crowd gasped as they saw the newcomer
carrying another sheep just like the two already
on the field – the sheep that Charlie knew as Alan
Shearer Two (Jessica Ennis-Hill).

Brains and Brauns looked at each other in
surprise. 'Well, I'll be,' Brains whispered, surprised
Neck Brace Man had made his escape. Perhaps he
was smarter than he'd given him credit for. Maybe
all three of them could run the B&B together!

Everyone turned to each other and started
chatting animatedly. Disbelief and shock and

outrage coursed through the crowd. Mr Hoskins led a group of Ovwick Rumble farmers and marched over to where Charlie was standing with his family. 'What's your game?' he demanded. 'You're trying to fleece us!'

Charlie's dad folded his arms. 'Now, hang on—'

'It's a fake sheep!' the man in the deerstalker hat declared, peering at Alan Shearer Three (Maria Sharapova). 'I've just bid eighty thousand pounds for a fake sheep!'

Mr Partridge held up his clipboard to call for quiet. 'Let's all just calm down, shall we?' he reasoned. 'I valued the real sheep a few weeks ago. I'll be able to tell which one is which.'

He shepherded all three sheep into a row – Alan Shearer, Alan Shearer Two (Jessica Ennis-Hill) and Alan Shearer Three (Maria Sharapova). Then he walked up and down the line, gazing at all of them intensely. The crowd held its breath in anticipation.

After a moment, Mr Partridge scratched his head. Uncle Martin grinned slyly to himself – he knew his spray-painting skills were second to none. Undetectable.

Mr Partridge reached into his pocket and produced a handkerchief. 'Only one way to settle this,' he muttered and spat a big handful of spit into it. He rubbed the handkerchief all over Alan Shearer Three (Maria Sharapova).

The crowd let out a gasp as, slowly, the black spray-paint masquerading as markings was rubbed off Alan Shearer Three (Maria Sharapova)'s fleece.

'I knew it!' the man in the deerstalker hat cried.

'Hang on a moment,' Mr Partridge stated. 'I'm not done yet.' He moved to Alan Shearer Two (Jessica Ennis-Hill) and worked his handkerchief over her fleece. Just as before, slowly the black spray-paint masquerading as markings was rubbed off.

Charlie's mum and dad looked at Charlie, and his heart sank as he registered the expressions of disappointment and betrayal on their faces.

He hung his head, ashamed.

This was it. At long last. He'd been rumbled. He'd been well and truly Ovwick Rumbled.

Game over indeed.

CHAPTER TWENTY-ONE

Charlie stood there, aware of seven hundred and fifty-three people, his mum, dad, brother and uncle, Mr and Mrs Hoskins, Saul, Mr Partridge, an irate man in a deerstalker hat, three sheep and a sheepdog all staring at him, waiting, demanding an explanation.

Charlie gulped. There was nothing else for it. He was going to have to come clean.

He was going to have to do what Mr Partridge had just done and rub, rub, rub the lies away.

Trouble was, Charlie didn't really know where to begin. What could he say that would make any of it better? That would make anyone try and understand why he'd done what he did?

In the end, it wasn't Charlie who spoke first.

Uncle Martin let out a huge sob. 'I'M SORRY!' he wailed, tears streaming down his face. 'I didn't get round to fixing the potting-shed door. Bessie must have got in there. It's all my fault!'

Charlie's dad frowned. 'For goodness' sake, Martin,' he huffed. 'Will you just be quiet?'

Uncle Martin wailed even louder. Charlie placed a comforting hand on his arm. 'Shush,' he soothed. 'It's all right. I'll tell them the truth.'

Uncle Martin wrung his hands together in anguish as Charlie turned to speak to the crowd. He gulped again and looked down at his muddy green wellies, lost for words.

Charlie's dad folded his arms. 'Will one of you kindly explain what the blazes has gone on round here, on our farm, seemingly right under our noses?'

A murmur of agreement swept through the crowd.

Charlie looked up and stared somewhere into the middle distance. He couldn't quite bring himself to look his family in the eye.

'I set up the auction using a fake sheep,' he confessed after a moment.

The crowd all gasped in astonishment, even though by now they'd all worked out that this was *exactly* what had happened.

'Why, Charlie?' his mum asked, pained. 'I don't understand why you'd do such a thing.'

Charlie shrugged. 'It just kind of happened on the spur of the moment,' he replied. 'Those men turned up for Jimmy that day and said they wanted their money by the end of the month; I knew we had a sheep that was worth a lot of money. But there was no way I was selling the real Alan Shearer, so I thought, we've got plenty of sheep here, they all sort of look the same, so we'll just use one of them.'

Mr Partridge mulled this over. 'The markings were pretty accurate.'

Uncle Martin let out another huge sob. Charlie's dad narrowed his eyes at him. 'Let me guess,' he said, 'that was you. You always were a dab hand with a spray can.' He gritted his teeth in anger. 'How could you be so stupid?'

Uncle Martin hung his head in shame. 'I'm sorry,' he said. 'I didn't mean to break the law.'

Charlie shook his head. 'It wasn't Uncle Martin's

fault. It was me. I made him go along with it and not tell anyone. Don't blame him.' He shot a tight smile to Uncle Martin in solidarity.

The man in the deerstalker hat stepped forward. He looked from Alan Shearer to Jessica Ennis-Hill to Maria Sharapova. 'Right then,' he said, and he made to grab Alan Shearer. 'I'll be taking this one.'

'No!' Charlie cried, and he moved to release the sheep from the man's grip. 'No! She's not for sale.'

'What?' the man in the deerstalker hat spluttered. 'I've just bid eighty thousand pounds for her!'

Charlie shook his head. 'Have one of the others.'

The man in the deerstalker hat didn't half look miffed, but Charlie had other things on his mind.

Jimmy looked on in disbelief. 'You shouldn't have done this, Charlie,' he said. 'Any of it. Especially for me.'

'I just wanted to help,' Charlie said in a small voice. 'You're my brother. I wanted to help you.'

Jimmy started to walk over to him, but a small commotion at the back of the crowd stopped him in his tracks.

'Right!' a hard, nasally voice called from amongst the spectators. 'Get him, Brauns!'

Everyone looked on as Brains and Brauns powered their way through the crowd, barging people out of the way to get to the front.

Before anyone could do anything – before Uncle Martin could stop crying and wringing his hands and search his pockets for a rolling pin – Brauns grabbed hold of Jimmy and twisted his head into a headlock.

'DON'T!' Charlie yelled, running forward. His dad shot out a hand and caught him. He took him firmly by the shoulders, and held him where he was.

Eloise let out a small yelp. 'Leave him alone,' she said, though her voice was barely a whisper. Her eyes filled with tears at seeing Jimmy in such pain.

'Leave off him!' Debbie called forcefully. She started to totter over to Brauns, swinging her handbag in the general direction of his head, but Brauns merely shifted his weight, held Jimmy's head in the crook of his right arm and pushed Debbie away with his left. It was all in a day's work for him.

Brains squatted down so his face was level with

Jimmy's. 'I have to admit,' he scoffed. 'I think your little brother's really rather plucky.'

'You leave him alone,' Jimmy hissed, gasping for breath. 'He's got nothing to do with this.'

Brains glanced around the crowd, who were all watching, intrigued, as the drama unfolded. 'I disagree,' he laughed. 'I'd say he's got *everything* to do with this.' Brains sighed. 'Do you know something, Mr Rudge? I'm really rather tired of you not giving us our money. That's all we wanted. Just what's owed to us.'

He looked over to the three Alan Shearers – two fake and one real – still lined up in a row. 'If we were a bank, your family's farmhouse would be ours by now,' Brains hissed. 'But we're not a bank, son. We're much, much worse.'

'Now, look here!' Charlie's dad said. He let go of Charlie and marched over to Brains. 'He's *my* son and you can't talk to him like that. You can't threaten him.'

Before anyone could do anything, the blare of sirens rang out across the farm. Everyone turned to see a police car burst through the front gate and career onto the field, its blue lights flashing. The car screeched to a halt and two uniformed officers stepped out.

Uncle Martin pointed to their shoes. 'Disinfectant!' he yelled, but everyone was too busy wondering what was going on to worry about the rules and regulations of sheep auctions.

'NOW what's happening?' Charlie's dad demanded as the two policemen made their way towards them.

Brauns quickly released Jimmy's head from the headlock. As Jimmy gasped for breath, he casually ruffled Jimmy's hair, as if he'd just been play-fighting the whole time. He stepped away from him, whistling, tracing his toe in the grass as if he didn't have a care in the world.

'We've received a call, sir,' one of the policemen said. 'Grievous bodily harm.'

'I barely touched him!' Brauns spluttered.

'It was me,' a voice piped up behind them.

Everyone turned to see Neck Brace Man hobble forward. They'd all forgotten about him.

Neck Brace Man motioned to the policemen.

'I phoned you,' he stated, matter-of-factly. 'I wanted to report a crime. This man attacked me, and that attack has resulted in this.' He pointed to his neck brace.

'Grievous bodily harm?' Charlie's dad boomed. 'Don't be so daft! Jimmy's already explained he had nothing to do with your neck.' He pleaded with the policemen. 'This man's making it up. He said so himself!'

The policemen both frowned, looking from Neck Brace Man to Jimmy, to Charlie's dad and back again, unsure who to believe.

'This man has previous bad form,' Neck Brace Man said. 'I, on the other hand, am a respectable citizen. I'm an IT manager! Does that help?'

'If you need your computer fixed,' Jimmy huffed.

Neck Brace Man folded his arms. 'I can give you the names of two witnesses who were there on the day it happened. Both upstanding members of the community. One of them's a vicar.'

One policeman motioned to the other to join him over by the police car. They spoke in hushed whispers for a moment. Eventually, the first police-man nodded and they both walked back to the front of the crowd.

'James Rudge?' the first policeman said, placing a hand on Jimmy's shoulder. 'We're arresting you on suspicion of grievous bodily harm.'

'Oh, for goodness' sake!' Charlie's mum cried. 'He hasn't done anything!'

'We'll be the judge of that,' the policeman replied.

A ripple of shock and excitement breezed through the crowd at this latest development. They'd come expecting a spectacle, and cripes, they didn't half have one.

'No!' Charlie cried.

Jimmy hung his head, resigned. 'It's all right, Charlie,' he said. 'I'll be all right.'

Eloise was clutching her mum in disbelief. Jimmy couldn't look her in the eye. Charlie's dad hugged Charlie's mum tightly as she sobbed into a tissue. Uncle Martin was as pale as a ghost.

Neck Brace Man sidled up to Charlie as the whole crowd watched the policemen walk Jimmy to the car. 'You can stop all this, you know,' he hissed out of the side of his mouth.

'What?' Charlie shot back. Now what was he talking about?

'If you give me the sheep,' Neck Brace Man hissed. 'The *real* sheep. I'll call off the police.'

Charlie looked at him in disbelief. 'Are you serious?'

Neck Brace Man nodded. And then he remembered he was meant to be pretending to have a stiff neck, so he quickly put his hand on the back of his head and pretended to wince in pain. 'Deadly,' he replied.

Charlie looked from Neck Brace Man across the field to the police car. The policemen were handcuffing Jimmy's wrists together. 'What I'm saying he did carries a five-year prison sentence, you know,' Neck Brace Man added.

'He didn't do anything!' Charlie protested hotly. His mind raced. A five-year prison sentence? It was bad enough when Jimmy was sent to Cleethorpes for two.

Neck Brace Man coughed. 'Time's running out,'

he said as the policemen started reading Jimmy his rights. 'Who are you going to choose? Your brother, or your sheep?'

He tapped Charlie's Newcastle United wrist-watch. 'Tick. Tock. Tick. Tock.'

Charlie gulped. Who *was* he going to choose?

CHAPTER TWENTY-TWO

Charlie's mum and dad and Uncle Martin stepped over to him. 'What's going on?' Charlie's dad demanded.

'I'm offering your son a get-out-of-jail-free card,' Neck Brace Man repeated. 'If you give me the real sheep, I'll tell the police I got it wrong. Mistaken identity.'

Charlie's dad looked very hard at him. 'That's blackmail! You can't blackmail us!'

The policemen opened the back door of the police car to shepherd Jimmy inside. 'I don't think you have much choice,' Neck Brace Man said.

Charlie's mum looked at Charlie. He could tell that she was trying to stay calm and bright for him, but he knew what his mum really wanted. She wanted both her sons with her, safe and sound. All her boys together. That's what she'd said. That's all she'd ever wanted. That, and a holiday to Marbella.

'Wait a minute!' Neck Brace Man called out across the field.

The policemen looked over at him in confusion. 'Problem, sir?' one of them asked.

'No,' Neck Brace Man called, 'I'm just thinking of something. Oh, what was it?'

He was stalling for time, anyone could see that. He glared down at Charlie. 'I'm going to have to press you for an answer. They're waiting,' he whispered.

The policeman had one hand on Jimmy's shoulder and one hand on his head to push him into the back of the car. 'Yes?' he called.

'Your brother or your sheep,' Neck Brace Man growled quietly. 'I mean, it's not difficult, is it?' He peered at Charlie curiously. '*Is* it?'

'We've not got all day,' the policeman moaned.

'This little boy is about to say something,' Neck Brace Man shouted to them. 'It's important to the case.'

Jimmy stared at Charlie in surprise.

'He's making me choose,' Charlie called. 'Between you and Alan Shearer.'

Everybody else looked confused at that, but Jimmy thought for a moment, and then a flicker of understanding crossed his face. He'd twigged what Neck Brace Man was up to.

It should have been a straightforward choice. Family was more important than sheep, even a sheep like Alan Shearer. But Charlie couldn't bear to hand someone like Alan Shearer over to someone like Neck Brace Man. It didn't seem right.

Charlie knew he was the only person on Earth who could help Jimmy, but it meant sacrificing his best friend. And all with what felt like everyone in Scotland staring at him.

Still. Family was family. He knew he had to do the right thing. He had to save Jimmy. Jimmy, who had returned after such a long time away. Jimmy, who had well and truly changed his naughty, reckless ways. Jimmy, with whom he had loved spending these past few weeks, like they hadn't done in a very, very long while. He'd just have to sacrifice his shot at the Young Farmer of the Year competition, that was all. Maybe he could take his chances with Muhammad Ali for Best in Show.

Charlie took a deep breath and shoved his hands into his jacket pockets, ready to announce his decision.

And that's when he felt them.

Four pieces of screwed-up card.

Charlie pulled them out of his jacket pocket and small silver filings scattered everywhere.

'What's that?' his mum said. Charlie unfolded the cards. He could make out numbers and pound signs on them.

'Scratchcards,' he whispered.

Of course. He was wearing Jimmy's coat.

Charlie could feel his face grow hot. The knot in his stomach suddenly felt like it had turned into a lump of molten lead, and the anger rose within him.

'You haven't changed at all!' he yelled at Jimmy, and he held up the scratchcards for everyone to see. 'First you started betting, and now you're gambling again. I can't believe it!'

Jimmy squinted to see what Charlie was holding. He opened his mouth to say something, then thought better of it.

'You said you wouldn't do anything to be sent away again,' Charlie cried. 'You said so the other night. But you won Eddie the Eagle in a bet—'

'WHAT?' Charlie's dad spluttered, but Charlie ignored him and ploughed on.

'—and you've gone back to your old ways and started gambling. You just couldn't help yourself, could you?'

Jimmy muttered something, but it was inaudible from the other side of the field. Charlie could see the pain and heartache etched on his face, but at that moment in time, he didn't feel sorry for Jimmy at all. Just angry. Angry that he'd been lied to. Angry that Jimmy had been so stupid. Angry at himself for believing that Jimmy had changed. Had *wanted* to change.

Charlie turned to the man in the neck brace. 'No,' he stated, loud and firm.

'No?' Neck Brace Man said. He wasn't sure he'd heard properly. 'No?'

'You can't have her,' Charlie said. 'Alan Shearer's mine, and that's all there is to it.'

Neck Brace Man looked from Charlie to Jimmy, to the policemen, trying to take it all in. '*No?*' he repeated a third time.

'It was my idea to fake Alan Shearer,' Charlie said.

Uncle Martin shook his head. 'But I'm the one who did the spray-painting.'

'Never mind that,' Charlie snapped. 'It was my idea and that's what matters. I didn't want to sell the real Alan Shearer at this auction because I wanted her to help me win the Young Farmer of the Year competition.'

Saul Hoskins folded his arms and glared at him at that, but Charlie didn't care. Saul Hoskins was the least of his problems.

Charlie addressed Neck Brace Man. 'But I knew that Jimmy needed the money to pay off you and Brains and Brauns, otherwise he'd go to prison or get his head squashed to a pulp. Or both. And Dad kept going on about wanting to expand the farm—'

'It's the flaming llama,' Charlie's mum butted in. 'I knew it!'

'But she's *my* sheep,' Charlie ploughed on. 'Alan Shearer is my sheep. And she's my best friend. I love her. And Uncle Martin does. That's why he hid her in the shed. It was what was best for her.'

Charlie looked Jimmy squarely in the eye. 'Alan Shearer will never run away on me,' he said, his voice loud and clear. 'She's not here one minute, buying me ice cream, making me laugh, helping me practise my sheep-shearing, then letting me down the next. She doesn't gamble away all her money. She's never once made me run from a diner without paying. She's never pretended that she's changed when she hasn't, and she's never lied to me – as far as I can understand. And she has the softest hair in the land, thanks to Mum's shampoo.'

Charlie's mum folded her arms. 'I knew it!' she cried.

'So of course I choose Alan Shearer,' Charlie continued. 'Because Alan Shearer never has and never will let me down.'

A hush descended on the crowd. Nobody really expected that.

Jimmy nodded at Charlie like he understood,

but Charlie could tell that even *he* hadn't expected Charlie to choose a sheep over his own flesh and blood. He let out a long sigh. 'It's all right, Charlie,' he said. 'You did the right thing. You always do.' He gave him a small, sad smile. 'You're the good sheep of the family.'

Neck Brace Man's mouth was hung open in shock. 'Are you – are you sure?' he spluttered.

Charlie nodded, just once, and firmly. 'I'm sure.'

Neck Brace Man shook himself, and then shrugged to the policemen. 'Well, in that case, take him away,' he huffed. 'And I hope you throw away the key.'

The policemen shepherded Jimmy into the back of the police car, the crowd watching on all the while. Then they started the car engine and zoomed across the field, whisking Jimmy off to prison for goodness knew how long.

Charlie couldn't bear to look at his family. He didn't want to be near anyone. To see the disappointment and pity and heartache in their eyes.

He walked over to Alan Shearer, smoothed her fleece, then gently led her back to the barn. Jessica

Ennis-Hill and Maria Sharapova, now back to being regular old Jessica Ennis-Hill and Maria Sharapova again, trotted along after them.

Behind him, Charlie could hear the crowd chattering about what had just happened.

He could hear Uncle Martin sobbing again.

He could hear the man in the deerstalker hat say, 'I don't want any of your blasted sheep now. Forget it. This whole thing is a farce! You hear me? You'll never be farmers. You Rudges are a joke!'

He could hear Mr Hoskins hiss, 'Too right. You'll never be welcome in this village!'

He could hear Brauns say, 'So I don't get to punch anyone, then?'

He could hear Brains say, 'I'll get my money one way or the other, Mr Rudge, you mark my words.'

He could hear Neck Brace Man say, 'And me. Don't forget about me.'

He could hear Mrs Morrison from the farm next door pipe up, 'What time does the tea room close?'

He could hear seven hundred and fifty-three pairs of feet trample back over the field and out of the gate, every single person tutting in disappointment.

He could hear one person shout, 'What happened to blood being thicker than water, young man?' but he didn't know what that meant.

He could hear all of this going on behind him.

But he didn't look back.

CHAPTER TWENTY-THREE

*I*t was a quiet and subdued night at the farmhouse that evening. Charlie didn't have much
of an appetite, for spaghetti bolognese or anything
else. Not least because his mum had wept at the
stove when she thought no one could see, and her
mascara and one of her fake eyelashes had dripped
into the spaghetti sauce. Charlie's dad was trying to
put a brave face on things, and kept moaning that
they hadn't heard anything from the police station,
and why weren't they being informed of what was
going on? Uncle Martin didn't say anything at all.
He'd stopped wailing by now, and was sitting at the
kitchen table, lost in thought. Not even listening to
his Michael Bublé albums could cheer him up.

Charlie cast his mind back to what Jimmy had said

to him earlier. That he did the right thing, he always did the right thing. That he was the good sheep of the family. Funny, but the knot in his stomach didn't make him feel like the good sheep at all.

'Thinking about the competition tomorrow, Charlie?' his dad said, trying to sound bright.

Charlie shrugged.

'You'll be grand,' his dad ploughed on. He looked at Charlie's mum. 'Won't he, love? At the competition?'

She gave him a weak, watery smile. Charlie's dad reached out across the table and squeezed his hand. 'We're not mad, you know,' he said softly. 'Even though you lied.' He knitted his eyebrows together. 'To everyone. And kept on lying.'

Charlie gulped. He hadn't meant to be naughty. He'd thought he was doing the right thing. But when his dad said it like that, it sounded *terrible*.

'We understand why you did what you did, Charlie,' his dad continued. 'But your brother, he's—' He paused, trying to find the right words. 'Well, he's just the way he is. I don't know if he'll ever change.'

Charlie's mum got up from the table. 'Excuse me,' she said, her voice barely a whisper as she struggled to hold back more tears. She let out a little sob and darted from the kitchen, her nose in a tissue.

Charlie frowned. 'What does "blood is thicker than water" mean?' he asked.

Charlie's dad bit his lip. 'It's just a silly saying, that's what.' He thought for a moment. 'I don't understand how you thought you'd get away with it all, though. You must have known *someone* would find out, eventually?'

Charlie shrugged. He hadn't really thought that far. He suddenly felt sick. Of course he would never have got away with it. What was he thinking? Of course he'd have been rumbled, sooner or later, and whoever had won Alan Shearer Two (Jessica Ennis-Hill) in the auction would come round demanding the real deal. All this fuss, and there had been absolutely no point in it whatsoever.

Charlie's dad caught the worry on his face. He patted Charlie on the back. 'You just focus on the competition, Charlie, and you'll be all right, my lad.' He scraped back his chair and stood up. 'I'd better go and check on your mum. She's — well, you know,' he said, and left the kitchen.

Uncle Martin shot him a little smile across the table, but it didn't make Charlie feel any better.

He didn't think anything would ever again.

In bed that night, Charlie couldn't sleep. He looked over at the empty camp bed in the corner, wondering how Jimmy was getting on in prison. The prison he'd made him go to. Well, all right, it had been Jimmy who'd got himself into this mess, but Charlie could have got him out of it and he'd chosen not to. *Had* he done the right thing? Had he been too harsh on Jimmy? Did four scratchcards and an owl won in a bet *really* mean that Jimmy was going back to his old ways?

A light switched off in the bathroom and Charlie heard footsteps padding down the hall and the unmistakable humming of 'Home' by Michael flaming Bublé. It was Uncle Martin's fifth favourite Michael Bublé song. The one about wherever you are in the world, all you can think about is going home. Because home is all that matters. Whether you're in Paris or Rome. Or Cleethorpes. Or prison.

'Uncle Martin?' Charlie called. There was a

pause, and then his bedroom door creaked open.

'All right, Charlie?' Uncle Martin whispered as he padded into the room and perched at the end of Charlie's bed.

'Uncle Martin,' Charlie said. 'About the competition tomorrow. What if I don't win?'

'Where's this coming from?'

Charlie shrugged. 'I don't know. It's just ... one of the reasons I chose Alan Shearer over Jimmy was because I want to win the competition. But what if I don't and Jimmy's gone to jail for nothing?'

Uncle Martin didn't say anything. In the darkness, Charlie ploughed on. 'What if I somehow go off the rails when I'm older, too? Like Jimmy did. What if gambling runs in the family? Dad already says I'm the bad sheep of the family for supporting Newcastle United and not Southend. I don't even know why I like them so much. I think I just preferred their strip when I was little and I stuck with them. And then you said I was a criminal mastermind. What if I go naughty, too?' He shivered at the thought. 'I don't want to end up in Cousin Graham's morgue in Cleethorpes.'

Uncle Martin reached out an arm and hugged Charlie tight. 'You won't,' he soothed. 'I promise.'

'I should have helped my brother,' Charlie said, wiping his eyes with the sleeve of his pyjamas. 'That's what you'd have done, isn't it? If you had to choose between Dad and Alan Shearer?'

Uncle Martin stroked the back of Charlie's head, trying to comfort him. But he didn't say anything. Charlie took that to mean, 'Yes. A big fat OF COURSE I WOULD, YOU IDIOT! WOULDN'T ANYONE?!'

Uncle Martin let out a soft sigh. 'You know, when me and your dad were younger, we used to fight like cats and frogs,' he said. 'All the time. And he was always nicking my stuff. He still winds me up, even now. Just a few years ago, he stole my Michael Bublé T-shirt and used it to wash his car.'

'What did you do?' Charlie sniffed.

'I accidentally left the iron on his Southend United shirt for too long.' Uncle Martin grinned.

Charlie couldn't help but snigger. He could just imagine what his dad would have yelled at that.

'But that's not the point,' his uncle ploughed on.

'The point is that I forgave him. For stealing my T-shirt. And he forgave me for the iron. They were only clothes. We forgave each other, because sooner or later we all do silly things. We all hurt each other, whether we mean to or not. And we can only hope that someone will be able to forgive us when we do screw up.'

For a six foot four man with a Michael Bublé obsession, Charlie knew that Uncle Martin didn't half talk a lot of sense.

He also knew that he'd made the wrong choice.

Uncle Martin gave him a little hug, then got up off the bed and walked to the door.

'That's what "blood is thicker than water" means, isn't it?' Charlie said. 'Family is more important than anything.' He let out a puff of air. 'I should have chosen Jimmy.'

Uncle Martin shot him a tight smile, then switched off the bedroom light and shut the door.

'But now,' Charlie whispered to himself, all alone in the darkness. 'Well, now it's too late to do anything about it.'

CHAPTER TWENTY-FOUR

Uncle Martin shut his nephew's bedroom door and quietly padded down the landing to his own room.

The conversation he'd had with Charlie had set his mind racing. He thought back to the day he'd caught his brother using his Michael Bublé T-shirt as a rag to wash the car. How dare he touch his stuff! Just because Mick didn't like Michael Bublé, there was no need to make fun of those who did. So Martin had retaliated by ruining Mick's favourite football top and all hell had broken loose. They didn't talk to each other for ages.

But then, after a few weeks of the silent treatment, they both realized they were fighting over nothing.

It was just a T-shirt. It was just a football shirt. It was just *stuff*. They weren't really important, not in the grand scheme of things.

Family was what was important.

Martin looked around his bedroom. He took in the Michael Bublé posters on the walls. His signed 2015 Michael Bublé wall calendar. His stacks of Michael Bublé CDs, Michael Bublé DVDs and a framed montage of tickets and programmes from all the Michael Bublé concerts he'd been to over the years. He couldn't explain why he loved Michael Bublé so much, but his songs just made him so happy.

And then his eyes fell upon his most prized possession. It took pride of place upon the shelf over his bed. His limited-edition-mint-condition-never-to-be-opened Michael Bublé doll.

He let out a long sigh. Sure, having all this stuff made him happy, but what was the point of having it all if everyone around him was miserable?

Uncle Martin gently lifted the Michael Bublé doll box off the shelf, and placed it carefully, lovingly, inside a carrier bag.

He snuck downstairs and into the kitchen and turned on the laptop. He boiled the kettle and made himself a strong cup of coffee, for it was going to be a long night.

He called up his eBay page, took a deep breath, and started typing.

CHAPTER TWENTY-FIVE

The sun was shining as the Rudges made their way to Ovwick Rumble Manor, where the competition was to take place. The Rudges minus Jimmy, obviously. And Uncle Martin, for some reason, for no one could find him. He wasn't in his room, he wasn't helping out around the farm, or baking more scones. His wellies and his fleece had gone from the coat rack by the front door. It was a mystery.

Charlie had woken that morning with lead in his stomach, and Uncle Martin not being there had made him feel ten times worse. He was the only one who had known what Charlie was up to, and had cared about Alan Shearer just as much as Charlie did. Maybe Uncle Martin didn't think Charlie would win the competition, and didn't want to be there to see the defeat. Or maybe he'd thought about it and realized that, yes, he was *so* appalled by Charlie's actions that there was no choice but to leave for good. Either way, it was clear he didn't believe in Charlie enough to stay.

Ovwick Rumble Manor was a country estate, like something from a period drama. 'It's all a bit *Downton Abbey*,' Charlie's mum whispered to him. The manor was situated on the very outskirts of Ovwick Rumble, and the sprawling meadow at the back of the farm had been used for the past fifteen years as the competition arena.

Charlie had been busy that morning, and he led a freshly shampooed, groomed, primped and preened Alan Shearer along. He clutched the rope tied around her neck, a somewhat less-well-groomed Bessie yapping at his side. Charlie's mum and dad followed behind. As they walked onto the meadow behind the manor, every single person from the village of Ovwick Rumble, and every single person from Bovwick Ramble, the next village over, and every single person from Fovwick Bumble, the next village to that, and one person from Great Little Matchely, four hundred miles away, stopped and turned to look at them.

Word had spread of the events at Argonaut Farm the day before, so even those who hadn't been there knew what had happened. They knew that this new family in Ovwick Rumble, the new family trying their hand at farming, had cheated. They knew that they had tried to fleece the other farmers by palming them off with a fake sheep. And here they were, as bold as brass, swanning into the competition as if nothing had happened. Trying to *win* the competition as if they actually belonged here!

Charlie tried to ignore what must have been a thousand people all staring at him, glaring at him, tutting and frowning and glowering at him. Instead, he took in his surroundings and tried to work out where everything was.

The meadow was vast, the size of at least two football pitches, and there was bunting and flags and fairy lights strung up all around it. In the centre of the meadow was a platform – a makeshift stage where Charlie supposed he'd have to stand with all the other contestants.

Dotted around the meadow were stalls and tables selling all manner of wares. Refreshments, cakes, hot dogs, books, candyfloss, bric-a-brac. Charlie was surprised there was any bric-a-brac left in the whole of Scotland after all the lots that had been auctioned the day before. He spotted Eloise, Debbie and Madge from Debbie & Dale's Dairy & Baked Goods Emporium serving all manner of ice creams from an ice-cream van. There was also a farm goods raffle stall decorated with bales of hay, a face-painting stall, a flower stall, a hook-a-duck stall, a splat-the-rat stall and the lesser known cuddle-a-monkey stall. Ovwick Rumble clearly made a big thing out of this.

And there, at the back of the meadow, was an old man standing underneath a small marquee. Charlie didn't know him, but he couldn't help but feel a sharp pang when he saw him. Written on the marquee tent was OVWICK RUMBLE'S OWLS AND OTHER STRIGIFORMES. Charlie didn't know what the last word meant, but one word stuck out like a sore thumb. Owls.

That must have been who Jimmy had won Eddie the Eagle off in the pub the other night.

Jimmy.

Jimmy should be here, Charlie thought. Jimmy was the one who'd helped him practise. The one who'd been there for his sheep-shearing and sheep-dog training. Jimmy should be here with the rest of his family, where he belonged. Not languishing in a police cell.

Before he could dwell any longer on what he had done, he spotted a man in a sun hat sitting behind a table in the corner of the meadow, with a sign that said REGISTRATION. Holding Alan Shearer's rope tightly, Charlie walked with her to the table. 'Charlie Rudge,' he said, trying to sound calm even though his insides were doing loop-the-loops.

The man in the sunhat looked him up and down. 'I know who you are,' he huffed, and he passed Charlie a clipboard with a form to fill out.

Charlie gulped. Was this how the whole day was going to go?

Once Charlie had registered, he made his way to the platform, where all the other contestants were standing on stage with their 'Best in Show' sheep. He recognized Franco from his school, who was standing at the end of the row of contestants, next to a small sheep with colourful ribbons woven into its fleece. Charlie gave him a little smile, but Franco's eyes were fixed straight ahead, focused.

Charlie took his place amongst the contestants, next to a little girl who had given her sheep a perm. Smack bang in the middle of the stage was Saul Hoskins, next to him a sheep dressed in a red bow tie and top hat. Saul glared as Charlie soothed Alan Shearer and secured her rope in place, but Charlie coolly ignored him. He had enough to think about without Saul flaming Hoskins.

Mr Partridge stepped onto the platform to a smattering of applause. 'Welcome, welcome, every-one,' he called, 'to the fifteenth annual Scottish Young Farmer of the Year competition!' Again, the audience applauded politely. 'We have here' – and Mr Partridge gestured to all the contestants on the stage – 'twelve brave young people from across the country, ready to battle it out for the crown.'

He looked around the crowd. He spotted the Rudge family in amongst them, and his jaw dropped in surprise. He peered back at the contestants on the stage until he spotted Charlie in the middle. 'Right,' he said. He smoothed down his jacket. 'Right. Well. I am the very model of fairness. I, as Head Judge, will not be biased. You can rest assured that yesterday's *shambles*' – he lingered over the word, frowning at Charlie – 'will not affect my judgement in any way whatsoever. All right?'

Charlie nodded vaguely, and that seemed to satisfy Mr Partridge, who looked down at his notes again and ploughed on. 'Let's get going, shall we? Round one.' He nodded to the man in the sunhat who had registered the contestants, and from the side of the meadow the man herded twelve cows towards the group. They plodded reluctantly into the arena.

Mr Partridge beamed at the crowd. 'Most milk milked from a cow.'

The cows mooed as if they knew what they were in for, and Charlie and the rest of the contestants gulped as Mr Partridge and the registration man started handing round the buckets and pails.

Three hours later, the competition ranking stood like this:

CONTESTANT	ROUND ONE Most Milk Milked from a Cow	ROUND TWO Fastest Time to Find a Needle in a Haystack	ROUND THREE Driving a Tractor Round an Obstacle Course	RANKING
STELLA RUTHERFORD	½ pint	21 mins 38 secs	DID NOT FINISH (hair singed by Hoop of Fire)	9
ROXY RUTHERFORD	½ pint	DISQUALIFIED (brought own needle)	7 mins 34 secs	6
LILY ROSE	1 pint	23 mins 41 secs	15 mins 24 secs	5
FRANCO GARCIA	DID NOT COMPETE (lactose intolerant)	34 mins 23 secs	DID NOT FINISH (crashed into 3 stalls)	12
LOLA JENKINS	¾ pint	18 mins 42 secs	13 mins 3 secs	4

ROMESH KAPOOR	¾ pint	31 mins 2 secs	DID NOT START (could not see behind wheel)	8
SAUL HOSKINS	1¾ pints	12 mins 3 secs	5 mins 59 secs	1
VIKTORIA KOWALSKI	½ pint	DID NOT FINISH (injured by hidden needle)	18 mins 30 secs	10
DAISY BELL	½ pint	16 mins 39 secs	DID NOT FINISH (fell out of tractor)	7
ESMEE TAYLOR	1½ pints	14 mins 2 secs	13 mins 2 secs	3
ANDREW GORDON	DID NOT FINISH (temporarily blinded by milk squirting in eye)	52 mins 3 secs	52 mins 3 secs	11
CHARLIE RUDGE	1½ pints	11 mins 10 secs	6 mins 23 secs	2

Charlie couldn't believe it – he was second! He'd managed to negotiate his way round the obstacle course in a tractor, despite never having been on one before. He was grateful that, as the final contestant to register, he always went last in each round, meaning he could see what the other contestants did and use their techniques. It had worked so far. Second! Only one person stood in his way – Saul Hoskins.

And now, this was it. There was only one round left. It *had* to be Best in Show. It *had* to be. It was always the final round – Mr Partridge had said so himself. Best in Show had been the final round for the past fourteen years of the competition, else why had everyone brought their best sheep with them?

As all the contestants filed back onto the stage and lined up in front of the crowd, they were reunited with their sheep. Charlie smoothed Alan Shearer's fleece. 'Nearly there, girl,' he whispered. 'Nearly there.'

The registration man handed Mr Partridge a microphone, and he turned once more to the crowd.

Here was a man who could happily listen to the sound of his own voice all day.

'Now we come to the interesting bit,' he boomed into the microphone, 'though I highly doubt anyone can say that what's already happened today *hasn't* been interesting.' He looked sadly at Roxy Rutherford, Viktoria Kowalski, Stella Rutherford and Franco Garcia. 'Crashed into three stalls,' he muttered under his breath.

Mr Partridge cleared his throat. 'Before we get to our final round, we're going to have a little chat with our contestants.' He grinned and gestured to them all. 'Let's find out what this prestigious competition means to them, and why they want to win this coveted award.'

He moved to the first contestant in line, Viktoria. A tiny girl with short curly hair, she nervously spoke into the microphone. 'I want to win the competition for my grandma,' she said, her voice shaking. 'It was her last wish.'

Mr Partridge placed a comforting hand on her shoulder. 'I'm so sorry,' he soothed. 'When did she pass away?'

Viktoria looked at Mr Partridge as if he'd just asked the dumbest question in the world. 'She's not dead,' she stated slowly, 'it was the last thing she said when I spoke to her last night.'

Mr Partridge quickly moved on to the next contestant, a big, brutish-looking child with hairy knuckles and a shaved head. 'And what's your name?' he prompted.

'Daisy,' the big brutish child replied. Mr Partridge shrank back a bit, and didn't even bother to ask another question. He quickly moved on to Saul.

'Ah, now *you* I know.' Mr Partridge smiled, and winked conspiratorially at him. 'You're a Hoskins, Ovwick Rumble's oldest farming family.'

Saul beamed proudly at him. 'That's me,' he replied, like butter wouldn't melt in his mouth.

Charlie wanted to stamp on Saul's foot or pull his hair or give him a wedgie, or maybe do all of those things. Anything to wipe that stupid, smug smirk off his face.

'And what's your one wish in life, young man?' Mr Partridge asked.

Saul pretended to think for a moment. 'Well, sir,'

he said, 'my very best wish for life is of course for world peace. I just want everyone to be happy.'

All the adults in the crowd went, 'Ooooooh!' and, 'Ahhhhhhh!' at that and broke out into applause.

'Well done, lad,' Mr Partridge said, and winked again. He moved on to the next boy in line. The other contestants obviously thought that Saul was on to a winner, because whenever Mr Partridge asked them what they most wanted in life, they all – ALL – said 'World peace'.

Charlie rolled his eyes. He doubted half of them knew what they were saying, but the adults were all fooled.

'World peace,' Andrew Gordon declared.

'World peace,' Romesh Kapoor mimicked angelically.

'World peas,' Lily Rose stated. When nobody applauded, she realized what she'd said. 'Uh, peace!' she cried. 'I meant peace. Not peas! World peace!'

'Hooray!' the audience cried and broke into applause once more.

Then it was Charlie's turn. Mr Partridge rounded on him, holding the microphone right up to his face.

'And . . . *you*?' he enquired. 'What do you want?'

Charlie sighed. Despite Mr Partridge's vow that he wouldn't let yesterday's shambles of a sheep auction affect his judgement, Charlie could tell by the tone of his voice that he was properly annoyed by all that had gone on at Argonaut Farm.

'To turn back time,' Charlie stated quietly.

Mr Partridge leaned forward. 'What?' he boomed. 'Speak up!'

Charlie took the microphone from Mr Partridge. 'I said,' he yelled into it, loud and clear, 'I wish I could turn back time. I wish I could have saved my brother. I wish I hadn't done what I did.'

There was a sort of stunned silence from the crowd as the words sank in. Charlie could see his mum and dad look at each other. In the hush, he could hear the wind blow. A ball of hay from the raffle stall silently tumbled past. Charlie let out a sigh. 'Or, you know, world peace,' he said.

Mr Partridge grappled the microphone back off him. 'Right,' he muttered into it. 'Very good. Very good. Let's get on with it, shall we? We've not got all day.' He reached into the pocket of his jacket. 'Turn back time,' he muttered to himself. 'Whatever next.'

He drew out an envelope from the inside pocket of his jacket. 'This year's final round!' he said to the crowd, resuming an air of pomp and ceremony once more. Everyone chatted excitedly as Mr Partridge brandished the envelope before them.

'Please be Best in Show,' Charlie whispered to himself, crossing his fingers in hope. 'Please be Best in Show. Please be Best in Show.' He didn't know why he was so nervous. He *knew* it was going to be Best in Show, like it always was. Everything had been leading up to this moment.

'This year's final round is . . .' Mr Partridge repeated as he opened the envelope and read the piece of card inside.

'. . . SHEEP-SHEARING!'

The crowd all gasped in amazement at this unexpected development. 'Sheep-shearing!' they muttered. 'It's never been sheep shearing before!'

'WHAT?' Charlie cried, astounded. 'What happened to Best in Show?'

Mr Partridge shrugged and tapped the envelope.

'That's what it says,' he stated matter-of-factly. 'Sheep-shearing.' He turned to walk off the stage, but not before Charlie noticed Mr Partridge winking at Saul.

Saul was rubbing his hands in delight. 'Sheep-shearing!' he was saying excitedly to the contestant next to him. 'I've been practising for sheep-shearing all month! I'm the fastest person I know.'

Charlie looked to the crowd, where he saw Mr Hoskins sidle up to Mr Partridge and shake his hand. The cheating so-and-sos! The final round had *always* been Best in Show, always! Mr Partridge had said so himself. There was no way Charlie wasn't going to win Best in Show with Alan Shearer by his side. But now, well, now it was obvious that Mr Hoskins had bribed Mr Partridge to make sheep-shearing the final category. And the *deciding* category.

What now stood in the way of Charlie and that coveted title of Scottish Young Farmer of the Year was Saul flaming Hoskins and a pair of shears. And Charlie knew what he'd like to do to Saul flaming Hoskins with a pair of shears, thank you very much.

'Places, please, everyone!' Mr Partridge called, and the contestants all stood behind their sheep, collecting the shears that the registration man was handing out.

Beside him, Alan Shearer let out a small bleat. Charlie thought it had a hint of fear, anxiety and disappointment in it, all wrapped up with a touch of melancholy.

Charlie knew how she felt.

'Places, please, everyone!' Mr Partridge repeated.

It was everything Charlie had been hoping against hope wouldn't happen. Everything he'd lied for, and betrayed Jimmy for, had been for nothing. Alan Shearer's fleece would have to go anyway, if he wanted to win. The very thing that made her so special.

There was nothing else for it.

Charlie gulped. This was it.

CHAPTER TWENTY-SIX

Charlie slowly stepped forward and took his place behind Alan Shearer, alongside the rest of the contestants with their sheep. The registration man thrust a pair of shears into Charlie's hand. Charlie almost dropped them, his palms were so sweaty.

'Is everyone ready?' Mr Partridge boomed.

The eleven other contestants nodded their heads, though Charlie didn't know why they didn't just give up now. This competition was Saul's to lose, clearly. It had been rigged so that the final round would play to his strengths, not Charlie's. There was no way Charlie could win now. What was the point? What had been the point in any of it?

'YOU CAN DO IT, CHARLIE!' a voice in the crowd rang out. It sounded like – no, it couldn't be.

Charlie searched the crowd in vain. There was no way that it was Jimmy's voice because Jimmy was currently under arrest at the police station. No thanks to Charlie.

'Go on, Charlie,' his dad called. 'Alan Shearer doesn't look like she'd mind too much.'

As if in answer to his statement, Alan Shearer trotted back a few steps and let out a whimpering bleat. 'You reckon?' Charlie shot back at him.

He sighed. All the effort he had gone to these past few weeks. All the grooming, shampooing and styling of Alan Shearer's fleece. All the spray-painting of her markings onto other sheep so that she could remain the special one. All the lying so that he could keep her. All for this now-non-existent Best in Show category. Her glorious fleece would have to be sheared clean off if Charlie was to have any chance of winning the competition.

'I really must insist we get on with it,' Mr Partridge said, glaring at Charlie and his family. 'Either you're ready to start shearing, or you must forfeit your place.'

Now Charlie was torn.

'YOU CAN DO IT, CHARLIE!' another familiar voice called out. 'IN THE WORDS OF MY FOURTH FAVOURITE MICHAEL BUBLÉ SONG, YOU'LL BE SOME KIND OF WONDERFUL!'

Charlie's eyes scanned the crowd of spectators until he found who he was looking for. His eyebrows shot up in surprise. 'Uncle Martin?'

And there he was. Uncle Martin, standing amongst the crowd, a massive grin on his face. 'I thought you'd left!' Charlie yelled. 'I thought you'd given up on me.'

'Never!' Uncle Martin cried. 'I just had to go and see a man about a dog.'

'What?' Charlie's dad called from the other side of the meadow. He looked down to Bessie, sitting at his feet.

'Not *that* dog,' Uncle Martin yelled back. 'Actually, not a dog at all. I meant, I had to go and sort out this one.' And he jerked his thumb to the person standing next to him.

'JIMMY!' Charlie yelled, and everyone in the crowd turned to see Jimmy grinning up at him.

He couldn't believe it. It *had* been him calling out!

Charlie's mum clasped her chest. 'What are you doing here?' she cried.

Jimmy laughed and enveloped Uncle Martin in a hug. 'I've got Uncle Martin to thank for that,' he said.

'What?' Charlie's mum yelled.

'HE SAID HE'S GOT UNCLE MARTIN TO THANK FOR THAT,' a man standing halfway between Jimmy and his mum repeated.

Charlie's dad raised an eyebrow and looked from Jimmy to Uncle Martin in surprise. 'Care to explain what's going on?' he said.

At the front of the stage, Mr Partridge tapped the microphone impatiently. 'Now, really,' he boomed into it, 'we haven't got all day. I must insist—'

'Hang on!' Charlie yelled at him. 'I have to find out what's happened!'

Mr Partridge was taken aback by Charlie's outburst, but Charlie didn't care. He looked imploringly at Jimmy, waiting for an explanation.

Jimmy nodded behind him, and Charlie saw three familiar faces in the crowd. 'What are they doing here?' Charlie cried. Everyone followed his gaze to see Brains, Brauns and Neck Brace Man standing side by side.

Except this time, they didn't look like they were after any trouble. Brauns was munching a stick of candyfloss, clearly in his element. Neck Brace Man was hobbling on crutches, clutching a plastic bag with a goldfish in it in the arm that wasn't in a cast. Brains was smoothing down his brand-new suit. In fact, all *three* of them were wearing matching brand-new suits. They were green-and-yellow checked all over, with leather patches at the elbows.

'What's going on?' Charlie called. This was all too much to take in. He felt dizzy. And not just from staring at their green-and-yellow checked suits.

Jimmy motioned to Brains, Brauns and Neck Brace Man. 'It's all sorted,' he stated matter-of-factly. 'These three gentlemen will never bother us again. Isn't that right?'

Brains adjusted the brass buttons of his green-and-yellow checked waistcoat. 'Correct,' he said. 'We're leaving Ovwick Rumble first thing tomorrow.

We're heading to the Isle of Dogs and opening our own B and B.'

Brauns look startled. 'I thought we said no Isles?'

Brains waved his hand. 'Details, details. The point is, we've got our money.'

'And me,' Neck Brace Man piped up.

'What?' Charlie's mum called again from the other side of the meadow.

'HE SAID THEY'VE GOT THEIR MONEY. AND THEY SAID NO ISLES,' the man in the middle of the crowd repeated. He rolled his eyes. 'ARE WE GOING TO DO THIS ALL DAY?'

Jimmy and Uncle Martin laughed, and elbowed their way through the crowd to where Charlie's mum and dad were standing.

Charlie's mum threw her arms round Jimmy's neck. 'Oh, darling, we were so worried!'

Charlie's dad, however, eyed him suspiciously. 'You were saying,' he muttered. 'The money. How come?'

Jimmy patted Uncle Martin on the back. 'Because I have the best family in the world,

Dad, that's how come.'

He looked over to Charlie and gave him the thumbs up. That just confused Charlie even more. He'd been *terrible* family. He'd put Jimmy in jail.

'I only did what anyone would do, really,' Uncle Martin said slowly. 'After I'd come to my senses. And it's not just me you have to thank. It's Michael Bublé.'

Charlie's dad stared at him, dumbfounded. 'What are you talking about?'

Mr Partridge rubbed his temples. 'We do need to crack on,' he called.

But the whole crowd turned to him and went 'SHHHHHHHHHHHH!' because this was the most dramatic thing that had ever happened in Ovwick Rumble. It beat the last most dramatic thing to happen – when Ovwick Rumble got a new mobile library stocking a whopping seventeen books, and only sixteen of them were the same title – by far. They were damned if they weren't going to watch *this* drama unfold before their very eyes.

'Uncle Martin bailed me out,' Jimmy explained. 'He came to the police station this morning, along with this guy.' Jimmy nodded to Neck Brace Man. 'And he agreed to drop the charges against me. Said he'd made a mistake. Identified the wrong man.'

Neck Brace Man shifted uneasily on the spot. Partly because he felt sheepish about how he'd behaved, and partly because he still had two broken limbs. 'It was the witness's mistake, really,' he mumbled. 'Stupid vicar.'

Charlie still didn't understand what was going on.

But Charlie's dad had worked out what had happened. 'So, basically,' he said slowly, and Charlie could practically see his mind whirring, 'Martin paid off this Neck Brace Man, and he agreed to drop the charges in return?'

Uncle Martin narrowed his eyes at Neck Brace Man.

'Not *exactly*,' Neck Brace Man muttered. 'Martin asked me how I came to have possession of the other fake sheep at the auction. He explained to me how it was better for me to drop the charges and forget about this whole sorry business. Something about trespassing and attempting to steal private property.'

He stared down at the ground. 'I've not covered myself in glory, I admit.'

Uncle Martin looked over his three-piece suit. 'No, you've covered yourself in checks.'

Neck Brace Man grinned. 'I bought this myself.'

Charlie's dad looked Brains and Brauns up and down, and took in *their* matching green-and-yellow checked suits. 'I'm guessing he paid you off, though.'

They nodded. 'We have been fully compensated,' Brains clarified, 'and will no longer be turning up at Argonaut Farm, that is correct.'

'We're opening a B and B—' Brauns repeated.

'Yes, I got that,' Charlie's dad interrupted. 'But what I want to know is where Martin got the money from?' A sudden thought occurred to him. 'Not the tea room!' he cried. 'You've not been nicking money from the till?'

Uncle Martin looked at him, crushed. 'How could you ever think such a thing?'

Charlie's dad folded his arms. 'Well, where did you get the money from, then?'

Uncle Martin sighed. 'My limited-edition-mint-condition-never-been-opened Michael Bublé doll,' he said, as if that explained everything. 'I sold it,' he added, which did.

Charlie's mum clapped her hand to her mouth. 'You never! But you love that thing.'

Uncle Martin shrugged. 'Not as much as I love my family,' he said. His eyes glistened with tears. 'No matter how long I kept it, no matter how much it increased in value over time, no matter how much I love Michael Bublé, it just wasn't as important as seeing you all happy.'

'That's where you were this morning?' Charlie called from the stage. Relief flooded through him. It hadn't been because Uncle Martin hated him for what he did.

His uncle nodded. 'I was up all night on eBay trying to find a buyer. Then, eventually, I got a bite. User ILOVEMBUBL3 bought it for twenty grand. Enough to pay off this lot *and* expand the tea room.'

He looked around the crowd until his eyes fell on Debbie from Debbie & Dale's Dairy & Baked Goods Emporium, watching from the counter of the ice-cream van with Madge and Eloise. She looked a bit shifty as Uncle Martin was speaking.

Eloise thought for a moment. 'ILOVEMBUBL3?' she said. 'Mum, that's you!'

Debbie looked at the ground. 'Yeah,' she stuttered. 'About that. We're going to have to remortgage.' Her face flushed. 'But it's a limited-edition-mint-condition-never-been-opened Michael Bublé doll. It'll be worth it over time, you'll see.'

Eloise smiled. All she cared about was that Jimmy was home, safe and sound.

Mr Rudge shook his head in disbelief. 'I can't believe you'd do that, Martin,' he said. 'For us.'

Uncle Martin wiped tears from his eyes. 'Like I said, family's more important.' He flung an arm round Mick's shoulder. 'My brother is more important to me than Bublé. No matter how many albums he makes.'

His brother burst out laughing and returned his hug. 'Well, that means a lot coming from his number-one fan.'

'Excuse me!' Debbie from Debbie & Dale's Dairy & Baked Goods Emporium called out from the ice-cream van. 'I think you'll find my limited-edition-mint-condition-never-been-opened Michael Bublé doll proves that *I'm* his number-one fan.'

The whole crowd burst out laughing at that. 'That's as maybe,' Mr Rudge said, beaming at his brother, 'but I tell you, I'm *this* guy's number-one fan.'

Uncle Martin looked up at him. Or rather, down on him, seeing as he was the taller brother. 'Really?' he asked, his voice a whisper. 'You mean that?'

'I do.' Charlie's dad grinned. 'I'm my big brother's number-one fan.'

That was what spurred Charlie on, really.

'*My big brother*,' he repeated to himself, up on stage. Seeing his dad hug his brother like that, telling his brother how much he meant to him, that was what Charlie should be doing with Jimmy. He should never have chosen a sheep over his own flesh and blood, he knew that now, no matter how much he loved Alan Shearer. All right, Jimmy made him run after wolfing down ice cream every now and then. All right, he liked to drink more than one pint of beer of an evening. All right, he occasionally rocked up in the middle of the night with an owl attached to his arm.

But he was his brother. His only brother.

And blood is thicker than water.

'I'm ready!' Charlie cried, standing firmly behind Alan Shearer, grasping the pair of shears in his hand. 'Let's do this!'

CHAPTER TWENTY-SEVEN

Mr Partridge looked over to Charlie, startled. 'Really?' he cried.

Charlie nodded, and Mr Partridge gestured to the crowd. 'Then, this is it!' he boomed, and everyone turned their attention back to the contestants on stage.

'Are you sure?' Jimmy called. 'Like, really sure?'

Charlie grinned back at him. 'I'm sorry I made you spend a night in jail,' he called back. 'But I'm gonna make it up to you. I'm gonna win this competition and prove that I'm the best farmer in Scotland.'

'Fat chance,' Saul Hoskins grumbled. The glint of the sun reflecting off his shears matched the maniacal glint in his eye.

'I didn't want to sell Alan Shearer,' Charlie

ploughed on, 'because she was my favourite. But I was stupid to think she meant more to me than you did. Than you ever would. I was just angry that you'd got yourself into such trouble, and you'd started gambling again and I was stressed that it was only me who could bail you out. But, well, now, this is the least I can do. Sorry, Alan.'

He looked down at the sheep, but she didn't move. She didn't bleat, or whimper, or anything.

'I don't reckon she minds, Charlie!' Uncle Martin called through the crowd.

Charlie held up his left wrist for everyone to see, and pointed to his watch. 'It's Newcastle United,' he stated.

Mr Partridge looked at him like he'd grown another head. Really he was just wishing this whole business could be done with so he could head over to the cake stall and make a dent in the Victoria sponge. 'And?' he sighed.

'And it's still a watch,' Charlie replied. 'It works just as well as a Cartier or a Rolex or any other fancy watch. Or a Southend United one. It tells the time, just like all the others.'

Mr Partridge looked up to the heavens, exasperated. 'Do you have a point?'

Charlie nodded. 'My point is, why do we place such value on some things and not on others? Why do we think we should pay more for a fancy watch than for my Newcastle United one when they do exactly the same job? Why is Alan Shearer worth eighty thousand pounds when David Beckham or Jessica Ennis-Hill or Maria Sharapova or Muhammad Ali aren't?'

A few people in the crowd started nodding in agreement.

'Wool is wool,' Charlie stated. 'What does it matter whether the wool has come from a Blackface ewe or a bog-standard normal one? It still goes into making mattresses and blankets and suits and' – he thought for a moment – 'other things made out of wool,' he added. He exhaled loudly. 'These past few weeks have been madness. People trying to steal Alan Shearer because of what she's worth. Because of her markings. Because of the quality of her fleece. She's exactly the same on the inside as every other sheep.'

He looked down at Alan Shearer. 'No offence.'

Alan Shearer still didn't make a sound, but stood there placidly. It was almost as if she had accepted her fate.

Charlie's mum, dad, Jimmy, Uncle Martin, Mr Hoskins, the man in the deerstalker hat, Brains, Brauns and Neck Brace Man all looked a bit sheepish at that. As if they knew that there was an element of truth in what Charlie was saying.

'*I'm* exactly the same on the inside as anyone else, despite all my freckles,' Charlie ploughed on. He saw Franco blush at that. So did a few other children from his school who were amongst the crowd.

'And Alan Shearer's still my best friend, with or without her fleece,' Charlie stated. From the corner of his eye, he caught Saul laughing at him, but that just made him all the more determined.

'So, here goes,' he said. 'I'm ready.' He manoeuvred Alan Shearer into first position, so she was propped up on her bottom, and used his knees to hold her in place. Then he took a deep breath, and nodded to Mr Partridge, who nodded to the registration man, who nodded to some random chap in the crowd with a stopwatch.

'Finally!' Mr Partridge cried. 'Fastest time to shear a sheep!'

The crowd all surged forward in anticipation. 'In three . . . two . . . one . . . SHEAR!'

All twelve contestants started to shear furiously. Tufts of fleece flew through the air. The sheep bleated away as their owners worked at them, clipping here, snipping there. The crowd clapped along in appreciation.

'Come on, Charlie!' Jimmy called. 'Keep going! Remember what I taught you!'

Charlie remembered what Jimmy had said when they'd practised the other day. *Just keep calm. Keep breathing. Concentrate. And don't think about biscuits.*

He wiped the sweat off his brow and ploughed on. The front half of Alan Shearer was completely bald. A small mound of fleece had formed round her body. Charlie knew he couldn't stop and battled on. Clip clip.

'Chop chop!' Uncle Martin called, but from him it sounded more like he was telling Charlie to hurry up rather than chop away. 'In the words of my first favourite Michael Bublé song, hold on!'

From the corner of his eye, Charlie could see a couple of the contestants slowing down. One had stopped altogether, and was sitting crying amidst a pile of fleece on the floor. Two contestants were flexing their hands, sore from clutching the shears.

In the middle of the stage, Charlie could make out Saul Hoskins working away. Most of his sheep had been shorn. There were only the hind legs to go!

Charlie battled on, faster, faster. Clip chop. Chop clip. Shearing, shearing away.

'Come on, Charlie!' his mum and dad cried in unison. 'Don't stop! You can do it!'

He was almost there. Charlie just had one hind leg to go.

'Come on, Charlie!' Brauns and Brains called out together. 'Remember what we said about getting her in a firm headlock! And sorry about all that nasty business these past couple of weeks. But we really want you to win!'

Charlie couldn't help it: he burst out laughing.

A fleeting thought passed through his mind. How utterly ridiculous it had all been. An ex-wrestler and his boss turning up at the farm, threatening his family. A man faking a neck injury shopping his brother to the police. Uncle Martin faking the markings of Alan Shearer on not one, but two sheep. Four hundred and seventy-three people selling their unwanted wares at Argonaut Farm's auction.

It was *all* so ridiculous if you stopped to think about it.

And now this. Charlie battling to shear the unique, beautiful and beautifully groomed fleece of his favourite sheep in order to win a competition. Six weeks ago he'd have been happy to win a quid at the arcades down Southend seafront. He couldn't believe how much all this meant to him now.

Charlie clipped the last few strands from Alan Shearer's back and stood up. He dropped his shears on the ground and held up his hands in the air. 'DONE!' he yelled.

A mere fraction of a second later, Saul Hoskins stood beside his now completely bald sheep, dropped his shears and yelled, 'DONE!'

One by one, the rest of the contestants put down their shears – either finished, defeated or flat-out given up.

Mr Partridge nodded to the registration man, who nodded to the man holding the stopwatch. He clicked the stopwatch off, and waited as Mr Partridge walked all round Saul's sheep, making notes on his clipboard. He squatted down so he could look all the way round the sheep's hind legs, making sure that every strand had been shorn.

He walked over to Charlie and Alan Shearer. The crowd held its breath as Mr Partridge walked all the way round the sheep, looking over every inch of it. He made another note on his clipboard, and then moved to the front of the stage.

The registration man handed him the microphone once more, and Mr Partridge tapped it to get the crowd's full attention. He was such a showman. He already *had* the crowd's full attention, he was just milking the situation. For longer than it had taken Charlie to milk the cow in round one.

'Get on with it!' Mrs Morrison called from the back of the crowd.

Mr Partridge smoothed down his jacket. 'Totting up the scores from all four rounds,' he boomed into the microphone, 'we have a winner.'

Charlie's mum clutched Charlie's dad's hand, who clutched Jimmy's hand, who clutched Uncle Martin's hand, who clutched Neck Brace Man's hand, who clutched Brains' hand, who clutched Brauns' hand, who clutched the last of his candyfloss and chewed it nervously.

Mr Partridge looked over to Mr Hoskins and cleared his throat. Mr Hoskins gave him the thumbs up.

'We have a winner!' Mr Partridge repeated into the microphone. 'The Scottish Young Farmer of the Year is . . .'

The crowd held their breath.

The contestants held their breath.

The *sheep* held their breath.

'. . . CHARLIE RUDGE!'

All the Rudges gasped and hugged in delight as the crowd broke out into applause. Brains and

Brauns punched their fists in the air victoriously. The man in the neck brace waved his crutches around in delight.

And then the same thought occurred to all three of them at the same time.

The fleece. The valuable fleece!

Brains and Brauns dashed forward and leaped onto the stage. Neck Brace Man dropped his goldfish bag and hastily hobbled forward on his crutches. A mad scramble for the tufts of Alan Shearer's fleece lying in piles on the floor around her ensued. Wool went flying as Brains, Brauns, Neck Brace Man and, from the crowd, the man in the deerstalker hat, Mrs Morrison and six other farmers all bundled on top of one another to get at the coveted wool. From the bottom of the bundle, Brauns held up his candyfloss stick, which was covered in candyfloss *and* wool. You couldn't tell which was which. 'Oh, well,' he sighed, and started chomping away regardless.

Charlie couldn't believe it. The rest of the contestants swarmed around him, patting him on the back, jostling him in delight.

'I won?' Charlie repeated, still unable to process his victory.

'You won,' Mr Partridge confirmed, and he held out his hand. Charlie shook it heartily. 'Congratulations, young man,' Mr Partridge said, and Charlie thought he detected a glimmer of respect in his eye. 'We may well make a proper Ovwick Rumble farmer of you yet.'

Mr Partridge felt a tap on his shoulder.

'What the devil do you think you're playing at?' He turned to see Mr Hoskins glaring at him. 'I thought we had an understanding?'

Mr Partridge cleared his throat. 'I can't help it if this lad was quicker than your boy at sheep-shearing,' he hissed.

Saul marched over to his dad. 'You said I'd win!' he yelled, his face red and tears streaming down his cheeks. 'First of all you said I'd have *that* sheep' – he pointed at Alan Shearer – 'but you couldn't go and steal it properly, could you? And then you said you'd rig it so sheep-shearing was the final round, not Best in Show. You're a rubbish dad! You can't do anything right!'

Mr Hoskins looked around, his face flushed with embarrassment. 'Shush, boy,' he hissed, and grabbed Saul by the elbow. 'Home. Now.' He marched a still-wailing Saul through the crowd and dragged him across the meadow.

Franco bounded over to Charlie. 'I'm glad you won,' he grinned. 'You deserved it more than he did.'

Charlie smiled shyly back at him. 'Thanks,' he said. 'I'm sorry you crashed into the beer tent. It looked painful.'

Franco beamed. 'Are you kidding? It was so much fun!'

Charlie burst out laughing at that.

'Well, see you at school, then,' Franco said. 'We could have a game of footie, or something? If you want.' He gave Charlie a little wave and leaped off the stage into the crowd.

Charlie let out a contented sigh. He couldn't have been happier. He'd got what he wanted and he hadn't even had to cheat to get it. This wish had come true. His wish about his family had come true. Heck, maybe he *ought* to get wishing for world peace at this rate.

Charlie's mum, dad, Jimmy and Uncle Martin bounded up to him and enveloped him in a hug. 'You did it!' his mum cried, her cheeks wet with tears of joy. 'We're so proud of you, love.'

Charlie looked up at Jimmy, unsure. 'I'm sorry, Jimmy,' he whispered. 'About choosing Alan Shearer over you.'

Jimmy squeezed his shoulder. 'I won't hear of it, Charlie. It's all forgotten.' He looked at their mum and dad. 'And you know what? I promise I've learned my lesson. A night in a police cell was the wake-up call I needed, I swear. No more bets. No more scratchcards. No more gambling. I don't ever want to go back to prison again.' He thought for a moment. 'Or Cleethorpes.'

Charlie grinned at him. Next to him, his uncle shook his head. 'I'm the one who's sorry,' he said. 'If I'd sold my limited-edition-mint-condition-never-been-opened Michael Bublé doll earlier, I could have saved everyone a whole lot of hassle.'

'I don't know,' Jimmy mused thoughtfully. 'I reckon everything that's happened is meant to have happened. If you'd just given me the money to pay off everyone I owed money to first of all, well, I might not have stuck around. I might not have realized what a brilliant family I have, now I've had the chance to spend a bit of time with you all.'

He grinned mischievously. 'And I might never have had the chance to teach Charlie all he knows about sheep-shearing,' he added.

'Hey!' Charlie cried, pushing Jimmy playfully.

Mr Rudge beamed at both his sons. 'I reckon you might be right, there,' he said, nodding.

Jimmy gazed wistfully at the ice-cream van at the back of the meadow. 'And I might never have found the girl of my dreams,' he sighed. He grinned at Eloise, who grew so flustered she spilled the tub of Thanks a Latte ice cream she was holding all over a customer.

Charlie rolled his eyes. 'You have to actually ask her out, you know, if you want her to be your girl-friend.'

Jimmy smiled. 'I will,' he replied. 'I'm just waiting for the right time.'

At that moment, Mr Partridge tapped the micro-phone again. 'Ladies and gentlemen,' he boomed into it. 'I'd like to invite the winner to come up here and receive his crown. I give you the Scottish Young Farmer of the Year, Ovwick Rumble's newest farmer, Charlie Rudge!'

Charlie's mum and dad clapped him on the back and nudged him forward to the front of the stage. Almost in a daze, Charlie climbed the steps of the podium and bowed his head as Mr Partridge placed the golden crown on it. Charlie then turned and bowed to the crowd, who were all applauding wildly.

He thought for a moment, and then took the crown off his head. He climbed back down the steps and over to Alan Shearer. 'I reckon she's the real winner, here,' said Charlie, grinning, and he placed the crown carefully on Alan Shearer's head. The crowd clapped even louder.

'BAAAAAAAAA!' Alan Shearer bleated, clearly in agreement with this statement. And clearly pleased at this golden crown she *should* be wearing, rather than the newspaper hat Uncle Martin had fashioned for her a few weeks before.

Charlie gently took hold of the length of rope

around her neck and walked with her back to where his family were waiting. 'Right, then,' Charlie's mum said to the troops. She took hold of Bessie's lead. 'Back to Argonaut Farm.'

'I can't wait to get back in the tea room,' Uncle Martin added, beaming. 'I've missed the sound of the till.'

'I can't wait to practise for next year,' Charlie said. 'I need to improve my time driving a tractor round an obstacle course including a hoop of fire.'

'Charlie!' his mum cried. 'For heaven's sake, you've only just won! Why don't you allow yourself a bit of time to revel in your victory?'

He shrugged. 'There's no harm,' he said. 'I've not been fussed about five-a-side football for a while. Though Franco said he'd have a kick-about with me.'

Charlie's mum and dad exchanged a look. 'Is that your friend?' his mum asked hesitantly.

He bent down to smooth Alan Shearer's now-shorn back. 'Yeah,' he replied. 'But don't bang on about it.' From the corner of his eye, he saw his mum beam at his dad. 'All I'm saying,' he said calmly, 'is that I love farming now. I want to keep being the best farmer. And you've got to work hard for the things you want, haven't you?'

Jimmy peered down on him curiously. 'Right you are,' he said, grinning. 'On that note, I'm off for an ice cream. Wish me luck.' He sauntered over to the ice-cream van and, after a minute of blushing and um-ing and ah-ing, eventually struck up a conversation with Eloise. Debbie and Madge didn't half looked miffed.

Mr Rudge looked from Jimmy to Charlie. 'Right you are,' he grinned. He clapped his hands together. 'And on that note, I'm off to see a man about a llama . . .'

He gestured to the Ovwick Rumble owls and other strigiformes tent, where the old man who owned all the animals was standing.

'This flaming llama!' Charlie's mum cried, but his dad was already off, making a beeline across the meadow.

She looped her arms through Uncle Martin's and Charlie's. 'Looks like it's just us,' she said. 'Shall I do us something nice for tea? Shepherd's pie? A lamb hotpot?'

'Mum!' Charlie cried, and he covered Alan Shearer's ears.

Charlie's mum clapped her hand to her mouth. 'Sorry,' she giggled. 'I forgot!'

Uncle Martin laughed. 'I'll do us some nice scones, how about that?' he said. 'We've got some apricots left. And I'm sure we've got some salted pretzels knocking about.'

She nodded. 'Sounds grand, Martin. Sounds grand.' She slung her arm round his shoulder and they started walking towards the exit.

Brains and Brauns and Neck Brace Man passed Charlie as they made their way across the meadow, tufts of Alan Shearer's wool stuffed in their pockets.

'What about Plymouth?' Brauns was saying. 'I thought we'd agreed on Plymouth?'

'I've heard Southend's quite nice,' Neck Brace Man piped up. 'Why don't we set up shop there?' He thought for a moment, and then stuck out his hand. 'Do you know something,' he said. 'I've never actually introduced myself. Not properly. My name's Alan.'

Brains looked at him in astonishment. '*My* name's Alan,' he said.

Brauns looked at the two of them, his mouth wide open. '*My* name's Alan,' he cried.

Mr Partridge, passing them on his way to the beer tent, casually dropped into the conversation. '*My* name's Alan,' he said, his mouth stuffed full of Victoria sponge cake. 'Wonders will never cease,' he laughed to himself, wandering off for his well-earned pint.

Brains, Brauns and Neck Brace Man all looked at each other, and then burst out laughing. 'All this time,' Alan Number Two (Brains) said, shaking his head, 'we've only ever called each other Brains and Brauns.'

'Less confusing, I suspect,' Alan Number One (Neck Brace Man) laughed. 'Hey, you know what? Instead of B and B, we could call our hotel AAA. Triple A. What d'you reckon?'

Alan Number Two (Brains) frowned. 'It sounds like a car breakdown service,' he muttered as they walked away. 'We'll think on.'

Charlie hung back a bit. He pretended he was seeing to Alan Shearer, stroking her hind legs to warm her up, given that he'd shorn off all her fleece. But really he wanted to take everything in. He wanted to say a silent prayer and thank you to his dad and Uncle Martin's long-lost Great-Aunt Cordelia, whose death and bequeathing of Argonaut Farm in her will had led to them moving up here, and to all this. So much had happened in the past few weeks – so many crazy, ridiculous, fantastical things.

Yet he had done what he'd set out to achieve. He'd kept his favourite sheep, albeit now fleece-less. He'd won the competition. He'd found a friend, an actual human boy. He had his whole family around him and none of them were going anywhere. If anything, Argonaut Farm was going to get bigger and better, now that he had won. Alan Shearer was still rare, and Charlie's dad was talking to the old man about more owls and llamas and goodness knows what else. Probably a lion.

Because if there's one thing life on a farm in

Ovwick Rumble was not, it was boring. No one could ever say living with the Rudges was like living in a morgue.

Maybe they should phone Cousin Graham, Charlie thought. See if he wanted in on the action. Because Charlie was sure this life was far better than living in a morgue in Cleethorpes. It was far better than when he'd lived in Southend. It was far better than anything Charlie had ever done before and he hoped against hope it was going to stay that way.

'Charlie Rudge,' he said to himself, his voice full of relief and pride and excitement and sheer and utter happiness, 'life is precious indeed.'

ACKNOWLEDGEMENTS

If it takes a village to raise a child, it takes a team to write a book. There are so many people I have to thank for making me a better person, a better writer, and for making *Fleeced* a better story. Firstly, I would like to say a huge THANK YOU to everyone at Penguin Random House Children's UK for their support, especially Kirsten Armstrong, my lovely editor, who, alongside giving me oodles of encouragement and fantastic notes, takes me to lunch and talks of marathons and piñatas made for hen parties . . .

I would also like to thank Natalie Doherty and Sophie Nelson for their copy-editing skills, Becky Stradwick for her support and enthusiasm in the early stages, and prosecco in the latter, and Jasmine Joynson for telling me where to be and when.

To my wonderful J-cubed of Agents: Jodie Hodges, Jane Willis and Julian Dickson at United Agents, who keep things ticking along so smoothly, send the loveliest emails, and are uber-efficient in everything. Thanks to Emily Talbot, too.

My fantastic writing groups – the United Agents lot who meet in the Three Kings every now and then, thanks for your encouragement and feedback; to the LCC crew who continue to support and provide fantastic feedback for me, THANK YOU! To my writing partner-in-crime Harriet Gillian, thank you for being acers.

To my friends who continue to amaze me with how supportive and awesome they are – especially my gang of Southend girls, and my Wednesday Night Supper Clubbers – I love you all.

To Mum, Dad, Andrew, Charlotte (sorry about all the lying in this one) and the little superstar that is Lily, you have all shaped me into the person and writer I am today, even if you don't know it.

Finally, to Rik, thanks for all the support, cheerleading, inspiration, hugs, hummus and pretzels and most of all for being my Fabergé.